Kafka Sutra

Imtiaz Akhtar

ISBN-10: 0996653534
ISBN-13: 978-0-9966535-3-4

Something strange is happening to me. My character is changing and my head aches. I am beginning to see and hear some very odd things.
Fyodor Dostoyevsky. "Bobok," a short story

Suffering terrible inner torment I became a writer. Then year after year I went on writing and in addition to my inner torment suffered for the idea.
Soren Kierkegaard. *Papers and Journals*

Contents

The Trial of K

LIFE IS so full of bizarre coincidences that, when we actually face them in real life, and not in the life we lead between the pages of books, we feel as if the incidents have been copied straight out of a novel or commercially successful film. This is exactly what K felt that afternoon when he was produced before the Magistrate at the Sessions Court in Alipur, South Kolkata.

It was a big courtroom, spacious as a rice field. The interior walls were yellowish with a tinge of red at the base. The high ceiling, and the large window with dark-green wooden blinds, which had layers of dust and time on them, bespoke quite clearly that this was once a colonial court.

The Magistrate woke up twice that morning. First he woke up in his dream, then in reality. As a man, he was given to useless metaphysical speculations. He was absorbed for a while thinking if the real waking too was but a part of a dream of yet another actual life being led elsewhere, as in a platonic cosmos. What if we discover after our death that the life we led here on this earth was nothing but a dream? The whole of it, I mean. The Magistrate was as usual unable to resolve this conundrum, and he dropped it from where it had crept in his mind: that is, on his soft white Proustian pillow.

After breakfast, he left for the court.

The day in the court began with the hearing of K's case. The Magistrate arrived an hour late. The moment he appeared from a secret back door, the mob of lawyers stood up and bowed before him. Each tried to outmaneuver the other by stooping lower than his learned friend. The court master, who was well known to everybody as the Little Judge read softly: *K vs. State*. K was charged with various provisions of the penal code that dealt with offenses against the State.

"Yes, my Lord, I am appearing on behalf of the State," said a hunchbacked lawyer who was known for his brilliance; so much so, that he had earned for himself the name of Dostoyevsky.

"And who is the lawyer for the defense," the Magistrate said while shuffling the papers whose reflection could be seen in his brown glasses. Then he turned casually to have a look at the accused.

He instantly recognized K.

What happens after that is that a feeling, an admixture of guilt and shame, overtook him. What if others find out about it! What if the police discover it! Everybody would mock me. Everything that I have built up so assiduously will fall like a pack of cards. These thoughts revolved in his head like a loud bell. He felt extremely nervous, thinking all the while that everybody in the courtroom was watching him. He was being looked at; his every move was under the scanner of the anonymous eye of the crowd. The shame was becoming unbearable. He heard a whistle. A feeling of intense weakness and exhaustion took hold of him. He found that his whole body was revolving. For a brief while, he wanted to lie down quietly so that he could recover his strength that had suddenly abandoned him. He felt, as he shut his eyes sitting on his chair, that he was magically standing near a neatly made bed with immaculate white bed sheets. He felt nervous all the while. His heart was throbbing unnaturally and his throat had gone dry. A short but strong spasm of lightning flashed in his mind's eye, then everything sank into the pit of mysterious void of the well. It was at precisely this instant that the Magistrate fainted, as one would say, dramatically.

K saw all this with the sense of indifference that a superior displays when he stands before someone whom he considers inferior, both in rank and merit. He was escorted back to his cell. As he lay on the bug-infested cot, the past flooded from every nook and corner.

K and the Magistrate had met in the dining hall of their boys' hostel.

"I have heard a lot about you," he had said to K.

They shook each other's hands firmly. And K smiled mischievously. Thus began their friendship.

They usually spent their evenings at the village cemetery that was right behind their hostel. The fields were bristling with wheat. Soft winds blew, and the golden-brown crops swayed like the waves of an ocean. The air was cool. Butterflies and bees roamed as freely as they could. Dragonflies fucked openly in flight, making the children wander at the marvel of nature. The sun in the distance would become like the yolk of an egg, perfectly round and red. Carts, pulled by their bullocks, passed slowly on the grand trunk road. The farmers who carted them sat entranced by the glory of dusk, the serenity of rural air, the majesty of god. Once in a while, they brought the whip down on the bullocks.

One evening, as they sat, they noticed a crowd at some distance. A bier was being brought down from a tractor. They both rushed toward it. The corpse of an old man had been laid down on a pier of wood. They soon found out that this old man was a champion drinker who would rush to the *thek*, liquor shop, even on dry days. His nose was stuffed with two tiny balls of cotton, his eyes had sunk deep into their sockets, and his forehead had been smeared with paste of sandalwood.

A young man, probably his son, was wailing, *"aab kaun isko piyega."* (Who will now drink this?)

He kept repeating it almost like a tape-recorder. Soon another young man, probably another son, arrived. He too was drunk. He hastily opened a country-made liquor, *Kareena,* and poured it over the dead man's mouth, which was slightly open. And then three rounds of country-made pistols, *kattas*, were fired in the air.

Crows, pigeons and birds of all sorts flew with the first shot. It was followed by the communal screams of peacocks.

When the corpse was finally torched, a nauseating smell, the smell of burnt flesh hung in the air.

They both left.

Black smoke that was minutes ago a corpse, and a day or two ago a human being, rose melancholically in the air.

"All that belongs to the earth must necessarily return to it," thought K as he turned back to see the orange flames.

Children stood silently with terrified eyes near the bier. Bored men crushed tobacco in their palms.

The friendship was consolidated by three things: their profound interest in god with a small g, books, and sex.

Their virtues of selfishness provided the base on which they erected the superstructure of their friendship.

It was a Friday afternoon. The metallic road to the mosque was dotted with white skullcaps. The corridors of the hostel had fallen marvelously silent. The chirping of birds, which usually gets drowned in the humdrum of daily existence, was audible. It was sonorous enough to make K vaguely poetic and metamorphose the disgusting feeling of absence of god into a real benediction.

The silence of the hostel was punctuated by the following words: *Maro, Maro behan chod ko* (kill, kill the sister fucker). A young boy had been caught stealing slippers from the mosque. He was being dragged by his hair and made to face the law of god. The door of the common room had been bolted from inside. Groups of boys wearing their skullcaps stood outside. When the poor boy emerged from the room, he was soaked in blood, sweat, and tears. He soon complained that somebody from the crowd had picked his pocket.

"*Bhai mein jhut nahi bol raha hoon,*" (brother I am not lying) he kept saying.

The crowd jeered at his suggestion.

No one took the indictment seriously. The proctor's Maruti jeep arrived when everything was "settled," as the proctor himself expressed it to the warden. Later the same afternoon, the proctor entered an air-conditioned hotel for his special Friday lunch. He was greeted coolly by K and the Magistrate, who were accidently also eating at the same place.

K and the Magistrate had an extended discussion over the recent incident. It continued even inside the dimly lit bar, which had a red sofa with big holes in it. The bar was plagued with rodents. They were so big that when K had first seen one, he mistook it for a piglet. Later, when he told this to the waiter, he calmly said that this was such a big problem that no one had been able to solve it. The managers who tried to kill the rats would either lose their jobs or, worse, die in mysterious, inexplicable road accidents.

In one case, the waiter said, "The head had been crushed so badly that no one could identify the dead man. He was kept in the mortuary for a whole month, then his body was disposed of as per the procedure."

K and the Magistrate paid the bill and walked back to their rooms. The next morning, when K woke up, his mouth still was sour. It smelled of rum. Early in the morning while he was half asleep, when his mind had not yet regained its consciousness, he had tried to figure out the exact position that his still body occupied in the room. He realized later how utterly he had failed in this task. It was after he opened his eyes and surveyed his room that he realized he had slept with his legs toward the south: a sleeping posture that was forbidden in his hostel.

"You must not sleep with your feet toward Mecca," his mother had warned him several times. His mind was occupied with this maternal advice.

The day began as usual with an ablution. The chill water washed off the dreamy world that hung in his head.

Soon a group of boys arrived on bikes. They spread the word that a student had been shot dead. There had been a congregation of angry students near the White House, which was the nickname of the Vice-Chancellor's lodge. Slogans had rented the air: desperate, angry and full of calls to manliness.

"Be a man. Burn this house of ill-fame," a student politico had commanded. And the mob had consigned the White House to red flames. The White House had, within hours, become a deserted, dilapidated bungalow with charcoal-black interiors. There had been similar incidents of looting and arson even at the staff's club and the proctor's office. In a matter of hours the whole university had become an army cantonment, a Kashmir of sorts.

The state transport corporation bus soon left behind the cluster of identical homes, often without window, whose walls advertised drugs for sexual impotence, creams for breast enhancement, cures for insanity, B-tex, spoken-English classes, and jobs with call centers. After three hours or so, the bus finally hit the national capital territory. On the right side of the window screen of the slow-moving bus, he could see hundreds of high rises with millions of similar looking windows of plexi-glass panel. New and promising, they stood like mountains, like fate.

On the left he could see the old India, where buildings still share the same wall.

Both entered the dark room. K switched on the air conditioning. The Magistrate, delighted perhaps at the Gandhian simplicity of the room, smiled, which exposed his red gums. The first thing that the Magistrate did when the lights were switched on was to pick up the copy of *The Diaries of Frank Kafka.*

"Oh, so you are reading this book," he said while K washed the utensils in the kitchen.

"I have been reading this diary for quite some time. The last time I came here, I accidently forgot it when I left."

"I don't like reading all these people. They are so full of pessimism," said the Magistrate, while K wiped his hands with a towel and prepared himself to smoke a joint.

K did not say a word. He wanted to avoid any further literary discussion. That night they drank rum, ate chicken, and slept. K woke up very early in the morning and saw the silhouette of the Magistrate near the door that had been open. The Magistrate stood bathed in the raw yellow light of dawn. He was leaving, a fact K had forgotten but remembered now as his consciousness came back to life like a light that warms itself up and takes time before brightening.

They shook hands and the Magistrate left.

"We'll meet soon when the university reopens," he said.

Two days later, K discovered that there had been a theft in his house. The money that he kept in *The Complete Marquis de Sade* was gone: all of it. Nobody had entered the room. The only person who could be blamed was the Magistrate. Nobody apart from him had come. There was no direct evidence. No one had seen him. And who could have? The circumstantial evidence pointed the finger toward only one person.

K returned to his hostel after two months, and he soon noticed that the Magistrate was avoiding him. Gone were the days when they would sit in the open fields and watch the idyllic afternoon clouds pass overhead. K's initial suspicion was further confirmed.

K completed his course and soon got enrolled at the bar. For almost three years, he worked as a trade union activist. He earned nothing.

Police arrested him on charges of waging war against the State. There was incriminating evidence against him: books of poetry, pamphlets, and most importantly a tattoo on his wrist of the communist sickle and hammer. This was discovered by police while he was being stripped inside the prison.

The Magistrate recuperated and the trial began. K was found guilty of various provisions of the penal code.

"The marks on his body, the materials seized by the police during the raid confirm that the accused is a Maoist, a threat to the sovereignty and integrity of the nation," the Magistrate read from his judgment in K's absence.

The next day, there appeared in the newspaper a most precise and unsentimental announcement concerning K's death. It was accompanied by a series of animated photos where each box depicted the chain of events. The prisoner would wake up in the wee hour of the morning at 5:45 a.m. – he would be given 15 minutes to attend to the call of nature and take a bath – at 6 o'clock, he would be allowed to read – at 6:30 a.m. sharp he would be served a breakfast of *biryani* [This fact had been planted by the Public Prosecutor, as would emerge later from the stories circulating in the press. In fact K was served nothing.]. At 7 a.m. he would be given time to offer his prayers – at 7:30 a.m. the guards would open the cell – at 7:40 he would be asked to repent before a priest – at 7:45 he would be hanged – and by 8:30 he would be buried within the compound of the jail.

A Story I Found Inside a Bottle on a Beach

IT WAS said of Rahim-the-midget that the spirit of an ancient *pir* (saint) descended into his soul every now and then, after the sun would go down beyond those TV antennas that hung in every neighbor's terrace. Over the years, his home had become a pilgrim's spot. It had the reputation of being a local Mecca. Men who desperately wanted to have two wives without one knowing about the other, students from local Urdu or Bangla High School who were struggling to pass their English exams, plumbers who were bored and unemployed, struggling actors who were growing bald, or ageing bar dancers who watched a TV version of Arabian Nights and dreamt of good looking princes and marrying rich, all such people visited his home.

One evening a young, nervous looking boy who was chewing gum arrived with his mother. His mother stood nervously at the gate. Men and women from the remotest part of this city had congregated. Women sat down on the floor with their heads covered with *dupattas*.

Just then, the smell of incense stick hit everybody's nose. It meant that the Holy Spirit had descended into Rahim-the-midget's body. He entered his room. His daughter followed him. His eyes were rolled up. As if in a state of transcendence, his eyes had become a useless organ that hindered his sense of perception and compassion.

Rahim-the-midget's lips were moving. His daughter, with whom he shared all his personal grief, all his thoughts, mundane, trivial, eternal, and farsighted, sat behind him with a pot of red clay that was releasing white smoke.

Everybody watched Rahim-the-midget in austere silence. Except for the occasional coughs of men who must have been heavy smokers, nothing was heard.

The student and his mother were the first to be heard. Even before the student could open his mouth, Rahim turned to the ear of his daughter and said something.

"Do you see dreams where you see that you have failed in exams? You are unable to complete the paper, and a voice shouts, 'Students your time is up.' You get all nervous and wipe your face?" asked his daughter who was now acting as an interpreter.

The poor student looked baffled. His mother nervously smiled and looked into her son's eyes. Her look said – fool say something.

"*Bol na*," (say) she finally quipped.

"No," said the student.

"Subject *bolo*," Rahim-the-midget finally asked.

"Mathematics," said her mother unable to believe that what was actually rumored about Rahim-the-midget was actually true, namely that he could read people's mind. He knew what was going on inside whose head.

Rahim-the-midget handed her a paper. "Open this after twelve days."

Thus twelve days passed in the greatest anticipation. When she finally opened it, she found that the paper was blank. It further mystified her. Unable to understand the meaning of all of this, she decided to visit Rahim-the-midget as soon as she could. Just as she sat down in his home, a neighbor arrived with the shattering news of her son's death. He had gone to play cricket with children from the neighborhood and had climbed a truck. His hands had probably slipped from it and another passing truck crushed his head like a pea. The mother fainted. She could not bear the idea that her desire to kill her own son, her secret wish, had been fulfilled.

II

Rahim-the-midget's fame and popularity had first risen to prominence when in the early 1990s he had predicted the victory of Pakistan in the cricket world cup. Many people, especially bookies and lovers of the game who frequently bet money, pronounced him an ISI agent. But the day when Imran Khan kissed his cup in full public glare [Rahim imagined to himself like Imran that he was kissing his English wife Jemima] was when all his skeptics had overnight fallen to his feet to lick them.

Since then he divided his time between bartending and occultism. He usually spent the days carrying vodkas, whiskey and beer in trays, and the nights living the life of a mystic.

The bar where he worked was right near the main gate of Sealdah Railway Station. The narrow alley was occupied with vendors selling pirated porn DVDs, second-hand magazines related to science and pornography, fruits, *lassi*, cheap and glossy shoes, T-shirts, lottery tickets, alcohol, and aged prostitutes who stood with saffron vermilion pasted on the parting of their hair above their nose. It was a small bar with a high ceiling. The voices of men composed chiefly of students, accountants, clerks, pimps, bookies, petty businessmen, and army men with cropped hair and moustache hummed incessantly.

As a young man, once Rahim-the-midget had stunned the whole city for a brief while. One day, he was going to receive his midget girlfriend at Howrah Station. His cab broke down in the middle of the bridge. He stepped down. He paid the bill. He yawned. He observed the rows of trees, houses and chimneys releasing clouds of the blackest smoke on both sides of the river, which decreased in size as he travelled further from the bridge. The view was splendid.

A streamer passed below his eyes, he could see the two lines of white foam that it created as it moved like a mechanical iron-made beetle in water. His mind was caught with the thought that when as a child he travelled in one of those steamers, he would experience an acute sense of anxiety the moment the steamer approached the bridge. He had often imagined that the bridge would break like Marie biscuit and fall on the steamer, and all of them would die like rats. Just then he saw a man who looked like a beggar jump into the grey water of Hooghly. The ball of white foam rippled the moment his body kissed the water. It soon multiplied into a series of vicious circles like the scales of an onion, one caught within another. Rahim-the-midget jumped into the river to save him. And he did save him. A small photo of him appeared in *The Statesman*.

III

I first heard of Rahim-the-midget through a maid who used to clean my clothes. She had mimicked how, when he was possessed with the Holy Spirit, he walked and shook his lips. She had also told me about the fact that, before he became all of this, he was in jail. He had killed his wife. My plan was to talk to him about this and write a story based on it. I was hard of cash, and without money my mind was not working. Late in the night when I first spoke to him, I began by asking him about the incident of Howrah Bridge.

"How on earth did you find the news?" he asked me.

"Through people," I said without directly naming my maid.

"But, why did you have to jump into the river?" I asked.

"Look Mister, when a house is on fire, whoever can must pour water on it without bothering about anything."

"And what did the man say to you later. I think he was mentally unstable," I asked.

"Insofar as the subject of mental instability is concerned, I am not going to speak a word about it. I only know that it is beyond my mental providence to pass judgment on any being created by god.

"But so far as his reason for jumping into the river is concerned, I believe the reason is such that nobody will believe. He would see in his dream that Lord Shiva had announced that he would meet him in the middle of the river. He jumped in the river to meet his god. And I know a godless journalist like you won't believe it."

"How did you find out that I was an atheist?" I asked him in a tone of utter surprise.

"Through people," he replied.

We laughed. I thought I must first tire him out as a hunter does its prey before the prey, in a fit of nervousness and not knowing what else to do, quietly submits to its fate. I wanted to know everything related to his wife's murder. My day would remain incomplete without it. But I could hardly ask him such a question. Confession can either be forced out or be won. I, being who I am, could only win it. He had asked me to see him a week later at his home. We agreed. I left.

IV

Two days later, I received news that uprooted me. A young man of about thirty had entered his home with a red clay pot in his hand. It contained blood of goat, chickens and dogs. The poor man was sleeping and dreaming about an ocean that was filled with pure azure golden water. He woke up and realized the stench of blood coming from the pot. He instantly recognized the young man, Raju, as his brother-in-law. Raju splashed the blood on his face and ran away. The shock must have been unbearable. On hearing his cries, his daughter entered his home with the terrified eyes of a chicken. The room had become a pool of blood. Neighbors arrived to help them. Three hours later, Rahim slept on the cot and suddenly observed that drops of blood that had dried now stood pasted permanently on the wall. No water could wash it. And in a state of deep grief he predicted his own death within the next three days.

Some twenty years ago, Rahim was neither a bartender nor a mystic. He was a reckless man who enjoyed noise, smoke, alcohol and women. He drank much and debauched regularly. One afternoon, he had visited the red-light area of our city where women stand in long rows with melancholic painted faces. He saw an innocent young virginal maid with whom he fell in love. Every weekend he took her to the Regent Cinema Hall. On the third week, after watching a romantic Hindi movie that as usual dealt superficially with the burning social issue of prostitution, he asked for her hand in marriage. Despite the hurricane of opposition, he married her.

Two years later he brutally murdered her in his own home. The story of his crime had provided spice for the gossip-crime loving readership. Rahim had peeled her skin, chopped her bones, gouged her eyes, sliced her buttocks, ears, breast, nose, and the flesh of her thighs. Then he packed them in black plastics and carried it on a Rickshaw. The crime had shocked the whole city like a terrible dream. He publicly owned his crime, admitted that his wife was cheating on him. He had seen her lover sleeping at the same place where he slept, he saw him playing with her hair the way he did. This infuriated him and he murdered her.

The sad incident had divided the whole city into two neat camps. One camp, mostly composed of male members sympathized with him. They viewed latently that it was a fit case where the wife was taught a good lesson. Such being the case, they argued that even if the author of the crime was the husband, the punishment should be minimal. There were some, very few though, who wanted him to be declared a public hero. The members of the other camp, mostly composed of women and some men, demanded capital punishment for Rahim. During the trial, even the Prosecutor and the Judge, being who they are, which is to say male public prosecutor and male judge, secretly sympathized with his plight. He was, thanks to the secret wave of sympathy, sentence to a possible parole after imprisonment for twenty years.

After Rahim had spent ten long years in jail, a new jailor arrived at Alipore Correctional Home. [The word jail has become unfashionable among the penologists.] Rahim predicted that the jailor would have a son. And he did. Not one but eight. All at one go. He soon became the jailor's pet. Three years later he was released on parole, and the jailor wrote in his report that his behavior was "exemplary, worthy of emulation by all other inmates."

V

For three days he lay on the cot. He felt like a bored lizard. He tossed from one side to another and waited for his consciousness slowly to grow dim when all objects merge as when seen through dirty glass or translucent plastic. *"Ah, ah, ow, ow,"* he would utter whenever an excruciating pain originated in his stomach and then spread over his body like a drop of ink on wet paper. His daughter would come to help him. She would administer him some rose water with sugar and go away. But the pain did not die. He made all desperate efforts to rid his body of this body, which had become useless. It was a hindrance to his eternal pursuits and not a bridge. He recoiled with much effort at the thought that his pain and body had merged into one.

Now the images from the past troubled his mind. He remembered with painful clarity the day he had killed his wife. He had taken the knife from the kitchen and entered his room. He had seen his own shadow on the dark wall. His big hand with a knife in it, how it grew as he travelled toward it and tried to touch with one hand the shadow-hand on the wall. He appeared like a character from a Shakespearean play who was entranced by his own shadow and perhaps inherent villainy. It was then that his wife had screamed.

VI

His daughter, who was a famous storyteller, opened her notebook. She had won several prizes at her Urdu High School for narrating *Afsanas*. She read one that ran thus: once upon a time a group of birds had held a conference at an orchard, which was awash with the seven colors of the rainbow. These rich birds were weary of a life "of goods and chattels, of deceptions" *(Koran, Chapter Iron, Verse No. 20)*. It was decided by the birds that they should find a guide who would train them, instruct them and finally show them the path to the divine. The guide was selected, and thus began their search for the divine.

The journey to find the divine turned out to be far more difficult than they had imagined. The birds missed the comfort and companionship of their past life. They missed the idyllic hours they spent every evening near the river. How happy they were then, how content, like children, and how handsome! Some of the birds complained to the guide that they were unwell and hence wanted to retreat. Others said that their wives were sad, their children wanted to see them and moreover the monsoon was in the offing. The guide was an old, sober and wise bird. He always smiled at them and allowed them to retreat. The journey continued, the hardships multiplied and the company dwindled. Now less than a handful of birds were left.

The remaining birds found it difficult to carry on.

One of them finally asked the guide, "oh guide, you promised us that if we birds follow the path shown by you, it would lead us to the divine."

The wise guide smiled. The birds had reached a huge lake that stood surrounded by a valley. The silver peak of the mountain stood painted on the lake.

The guide said, "Look, *there* is god."

When the birds turned their gaze toward the lake, they saw their own image reflected on the surface of the water.

The moment this story was over, the content smile of a man who was not in the least afraid of death, appeared on Rahim's face. It was a Friday. At noon, the Imam from the local mosque cleared his throat on the loudspeaker before he began the sermon.

"Everyone who exists shall enjoy the taste of death."

"Each one of your actions shall be accounted for."

"The construction of the mosque requires more money. Please, in the name of God make your contributions. The names shall be announced the coming Friday."

Once in a while Rahim would open his eyes and see everybody around him. He still had two more days, as per his own prediction. On the last day, early in the morning, he felt at ease. He spoke much and inquired about the price of rice from the shopkeeper. The cloud of death had passed his head. Now it was sunshine. Everybody thought that his own prediction about his death had passed. He might have pronounced it, but it was in the heat of insanity. No sane man would, after all, want to die. His daughter had grown talkative, and she even spoke to me. Rahim-the-midget invited me to sit near him. He spoke to me about this and that, about his past life, about his wife, about everything imaginable, and then I left his house.

Soon he lay on his cot and died. It was six thirty in the evening when he died. A minute later the nearby temple played an enchanting *bhajan* (devotional song), and a group of monks – Buddhist, Jains and even *Sanatanis* walked the bazaar. The *Muazin* as usual cleared his throat and then called the faithful to the mosque. This was followed by an item number being played on the loudspeaker. He was taken without any pomp and shown, then buried under the lemon tree. Thirty years later when I will die, I would like to be buried in the same grave.

An Interview with Orhan Pamuk

I OBSERVED him carefully as he walked to the door. I knew time was running out but suppressed the urge to check my watch. I took a deep breath and started to count in reverse under my breath. "Ten, nine, eight, seven...." I was so nervous. The room was furnished in a red sofa and red carpet. I sat there wiping the dots of perspiration from my forehead. Just then I detected the smell of rose. To my utter surprise, I saw Orhan Pamuk standing right before me. He wore a light-blue shirt and khaki pants. His face was beetroot red, and his hair was silvery. His cool and calm demeanor suggested that he had spent years reading books. He was a man who knew everything about everything. If one removed the skullcap of this man, all one would get to see are books stacked up in a jumble and disorderly fashion. I got up with a huge smile on my face and shook hands with him. I had forgotten about my own miserable existence. All my nihilist thoughts had flown out the window.

The story of how I had met Orhan Pamuk that day had begun one month ago. Back then I was working as a journalist in Delhi.

It was early morning when I had woken up. As usual I had to lift the heavy brown curtain of my room to see if it really was morning. The windowpanes had been sprayed with the freshest dew. One could quite easily scribe Rumi's verses of love and separation on them. Just then I had received a phone call from my editor.

"You are going to get an interview with Orhan Pamuk. And for this you'll have to go to Jodhpur where he is coming to date Kiran Desai."

"But sir, when do I have to leave for this?"

"The interview is scheduled for this Saturday at a hotel where he'll come for dinner. And listen, you need to ensure that nobody misses the spicy details of his relationship with Kiran. It will sell like hot cakes in the market."

I listened to him quietly.

With a cup of café solo, I stood near my balcony. Men wearing ties, children wearing mufflers and monkey caps stood near the bus stand. A heavy layer of smog covered the distant buildings of Delhi.

I saw Delhi as one sees it in a dream.

Those days, during the day I used to be busy as usual typing stories and reading the breaking news emerging from newsrooms. Soon, my editor entered the office rolling the keys of a car in his index finger and humming a song.

Mr. D immediately called me inside. As I entered the smoke-filled chamber, he was speaking over his mobile phone while blowing a cloud of white smoke from his mouth. A dim yellow light was burning and a thick floating cloud of white smoke had gathered over his head. With his left hand he smoked cigarette and with his right he held his mobile. He turned his chair to face me.

"Yes, yes, I know that this summer we'll have to carry a story concerning the holidays spent by various judges and big-shot lawyers."

He looked at me and forced a smile on his face. He indicated with his hands that I take the chair. And then I sat down.

"So you are prepared for the interview," said Mr. D while flattening his torso on his chair and lighting yet another cigarette.

"Yes sir, but I haven't read his *White Castle* and *Cevdat Bey and his Sons.*"

"This is not how you are going to work here. You have to be laborious."

"But I hardly get time to read," I sincerely protested.

"You should have read both these novels."

"One of them has not yet been translated into English," I finally argued, unable to control my ingrained lawyering instinct.

Mr. D was now caught in his own game. His faux pas was evident to him as well. He looked nervous like a child.

The moment I stepped out of my office I felt free, like a prisoner who had just completed his term. I inhaled a lungful of chilled air of Delhi. The hawkers, the buildings, the densely populated parking lots, the dust-laden trees, the labyrinthine streets that resembled one another, those youngsters walking the street wearing colorful socks with slippers: practically everything was lost under the thick cover of smog.

I saw Delhi as one sees it in a dream.

In the roadside corners, groups of migrant workers with their heads covered with *gamchas* sat down in circles

to heat themselves by burning plastics, tires and sometimes even blood-stained sanitary pads. A long and dense
black smoke rose up in the air where the fire burned.

I soon arrived at Delhi High Court. I met a friend
from Aligarh. His name is Amique. Every time he sees
me a bright smile lights his face, his smile adds a smile to
my face, and mine to his and so on and so forth.

That day our discussion began with the usual who was
reading what, then we had a long talk over how immoral
the government had become in our eyes especially after
the latest hike in the price of cigarettes and alcohol. We
then discussed the girls of our college. We recalled who
was dating whom, who is still dating whom, who could
have dated whom, who should have dated whom, and
lastly those who should never have dated each other.

Before I left him, I told him about the dream I had last
week. In the dream I met Orhan Pamuk and asked him if
he could give me his original notebook of *Snow*. My
friend heard this and gave me a smile.

"So, you want to visit Istanbul and meet Orhan
Pamuk."

I said nothing. An automatic smile ran over my face.

Before we parted I told him about my scheduled
interview. On hearing this, he patted me on my shoulder
and gave me a big smile.

Like a typical suspicious lawyer who never trusts
anyone, he once again asked me, "Are you seriously going
to interview him?"

"Yes, this Saturday at a hotel in Jodhpur. He is coming
to Rajasthan to meet Kiran Desai, and he has agreed to
do this."

"Good luck to you then."

I finally arrived at Jodhpur with a copy of Maxim
Gorky's autobiography *My Apprenticeship*. Jodhpur, I must

confess, is a red city. Buildings of all shapes and sizes are made up of red stones. On the very first day I took an auto and arrived at the foot of a hill. I had to walk all the way up to reach the park where I had planned to drink a coffee, smoke a cigarette and enjoy a bird's eye view of the city. As I slowly walked, gathering my breath, young boys at the turning of the road appeared holding green bottles of beer. My sense of desolation worsened as I thought about Gorky's failed attempt to commit suicide. He had taken a gun and shot himself. But he survived to tell his own tale. Once I saw the Hanuman Temple where the triangular red flags with golden borders were fluttering, I decided to sit there and archive the city in my memory. I saw myself that I was sitting there, so I walked toward the temple and sat there. Once I sat there, I *saw* myself that I am standing and thinking about sitting.

I laid my eyes on the city below me. Miniscule rows of identical homes and cars appeared from above. Altitude somehow always impregnates me with strange and terri-fying metaphysical thoughts. I said this to myself as I lighted my cigarette with an orange-red sun before me. On my right, I could see the walls of Mehrangarh Fort and on my left a brown mountain range. The cricket sta-dium, like one colossal nest, stood in front of me. Streets lights appeared below me one after another like stars that appear in the sky after sunset.

I still had two days before me. I continued reading Maxim Gorky at a feverish pace. I was now reading the other part entitled *My University*. The next day I left for Mehrangarh Fort. As the auto left the cluster of houses, passed by a caravan of camels munching straw while drops of saliva dripped from their mouths, I took out my note pad. I had to prepare my questions. This was my only chance to do something I had always dreamed of.

By the time I finished my work, the blood circulation of my leg had clotted. As I tried to lift my leg, the pain rose, piercing it like needles.

That day when I came back I felt once again very strange. It happens to me. Once in every while I feel like an animal. I don't know how I should write this. I can't express this by merely stating that I experience self-alienation. This would mask a lot. I don't like reading books. I don't like meeting people. I just feel like lying on the floor like a snake. I hibernate. I shut my eyes and try not to think anything. I try my best to hide myself from myself. I shut my eyes and try hard to imagine a dark screen on the screen of my eyes. I feel like a tree that has just been uprooted. This had happened to me some time ago when I heard that Modi had won the national election. I had lain on the floor for three days at a stretch. Usually I get back to my feet in four to five days. But here I didn't have this luxury. I had to interview Mr. Pamuk, which meant that I must once again become a normal human being. I tried to regain my sense of being by getting cheap whiskey from a liquor shop. It made me feel worse.

I sat down in my hotel room drinking and smoking. I still had one more day to go. Below me life went on as usual. Men wearing big silver earrings walked the street. Carts pulled by camels wearing red, yellow, pink and blue bands and golden color bells on their necks moved about the place. Women wearing white bangles right up their biceps walked in the street.

I woke up the next day still feeling very low. But today was the day when I'd finally do the interview and leave this place. In order to feel normal I thought it was best to get drunk. I drank vodkas with orange juice. I kept drinking until I saw that my two right hands moved to get hold of two pens with which I tried hard to scribe my sense of desolation. It was already 8:30 in the evening. The interview was scheduled for 9:30 p.m. At 9 o'clock sharp I left my hotel and took the auto. I was there in ten minutes.

I entered the hotel and informed the manager about my arrival. The manager was playing an extremely affable manager. So he asked me to sit on the sofa near the counter. Ten minutes later he showed me a room.

So now, unbelievably, I sat before my idol.

"How are you sir?" I had said to him in a polite way.

I was greeted with an affable, fatherly smile. And we sat down on the sofa in matter of fact way. I started blabbering before him. He patiently looked at me with a perpetual smile spread over his face. I was so drunk that I started to speak about my own self. It didn't occur to me once that I was there to take his interview, not give him mine. I asked him just two or three of my questions from the long Wikipedia of my questions. The rest of the time I was busy speaking about myself. Maybe it was because of the alcohol or maybe it was because of my own excitement. Our conversation lasted for well beyond two hours. I shared with him some of my deeply held fears. One of them was the fear of not being able to become a writer in my lifetime. He listened with the rapt attention of a student. He sat comfortably on the sofa listening to every word being uttered. By now he had become a listener and I a raconteur. It was almost 2 o' clock in the night when I left him. The manager offered me a dinner with lot of booze. I was so happy that I couldn't refuse him anything. I came back to my room and slept peacefully like a log.

The next morning I woke up. I took my bag to search for the notebook so that I could file my story by evening.

I filed the story regarding this interview, mailed it to my editor and then left Jodhpur. I arrived in Delhi and then the next morning entered my office. Mr. D asked me to enter his chamber. He looked very angry.

As I sat he took the printed copy of the story in his hands and said, "What nonsense is this? Don't you realize what you've done? Where is Orhan Pamuk, Imtiaz? This is all about you. Do you realize this? Go and immediately and file another story. Write more about him and less about you."

I left with a feeling of exasperation. I thought I had written a good enough story but this man was just too greedy to let anything pass just like that. In the following two days, I filed three versions of the story. I woke up early morning and was busy reading *Soren Kierkegaard's Papers and Journals.* Just then I received a phone call from my office.

One of our office boys, Rakesh, informed me in Hindi with his deep nasal voice that, "sir wants to see you immediately *jaldi aao,* come quickly."

I left my home and arrived at his chamber. His wife who often competed with him in villainy was there as well. I had a printed copy of the final version.

She snatched the copy from my hand and started to shout at me saying, "Is this how you're going to work here?"

Mr. D heard her and he was now playing the good cop.

"Darling I am going to talk to him. Give me five minutes."

She fell silent like a well-tamed pet. I was shocked beyond measure and decided to hand over my resignation.

But before I could say this, Mr. D said, "Imtiaz I think you should take a leave."

It was his polite way to say that I had been fired.

I said to him, "But you first need to clear my account."

He agreed to do this at once. It was then that I left Delhi and came back to my city with the intention of perfecting the art of writing. If my interview with Orhan Pamuk could not get published, why the heck should I be worried about it, especially when I had the faith in me that someday I could write a short story about it and send a copy of it to *my* Orhan Pamuk.

Her Ideal Husband

ONE THING I know for sure is this! There is no perfect or sure-fire way to begin a short story. Each
story is like a woman: it reveals itself in ways that you
cannot fathom. I was explaining all of this to one of my
college friends who is a struggling writer. We sat near
Café Coffee Day at Okhla, while both of us sipped beer.
The weather was extremely hot. It felt as if someone was
blowing hot air on our parched faces. We started to drink
our beers at six. The sky in the horizon had turned
orange-red. The air carried dozens of balloons of black
smoke. In the place where we sat, a delicious smell of
steaming momos wafted in the air. What followed was
the usual: a conversation between two alcoholics. We
were talking about our college days. I still remember our
days. Sometimes, and especially when my heart is soaked
in beer, I feel as if I am still in my college. How time flies!
My friend often tells me that time is that wet sand in your
hand that you try to hold. The more you try to contain it,

grasp it, freeze it, own it, the quicker it slips between your fingers.

We discussed the so-called judge lobby. We were both in the law college, which was right next to the village cemetery. So, these guys, I mean the sons and daughters of judges, would come, and they would sit in the middle of the college and have these nice little conversations about how the numbers of judges from the lower castes had gone up in recent times. Or they would debate issues like merit versus reservation. These debates, to say the least, were one-sided. They were couched in the semantics of the corporate media and if you got caught in them, like we sometimes did, you'd die of boredom.

Then we discussed our favorite topic: girls. You see, we had some of the prettiest Muslim girls of this century in our law college. Their cheeks were pink without expensive blush-on. Their eyes, my god: if you looked into them for a few seconds, you would feel compelled to relieve yourself by hand inside a bathroom. As it happens in cinema, all these beautiful girls ran after bad boys. What attracted these sober girls to boys who frequently participated in actual gang wars between rival student groups puzzled me. It is still a conundrum.

We were not like them. I mean, my friend and I were students who usually arrived for the lectures at the last minute. We sat in the back row and immersed our troubled souls in thick books like *Anna Karenina* or *The Second Sex*. There were times when even our professors would notice (we noticed them noticing us) that we were mentally elsewhere, in a land beyond the mists. I sometimes remind myself that perhaps they were afraid of us. I mean, we were students who read lots of books and were referred to as intellectual types. We countered questions with questions. Who would dare to touch us!

II

The next day we met again. Like the preceding day, I called him.

Where are you?

I'm at my office.

When will you come?

My boss has actually asked me to work for an extra hour today.

Will he pay you for the extra hour?

We repeated our conversation. Ditto. Both of us laughed at this.

Later my friend came. I sat quietly and observed Sikh men emerge from expensive big cars. They wore some of the most colorful turbans I had seen: red, yellow, blue, and ochre with trident.

That day my friend told me a story about one of our classmates whom we both deeply desired but never approached for several reasons.

You know this well. Every class has a few typical characters. We have the senior citizens. We have the kids. We have the aunts and uncles. And yes, we have those who are held up as the model students. Roxanna was like that. She stood first in the class. She rarely slept during the boring law lectures devoted to procedures. She shared an excellent rapport with all the teachers. And she answered all the questions. Or at the least she would try to do so.

Roxanna was the model student of our class. If you did anything displeasing, the teacher would be prompt to remind you that you should try to be like her.

The model student was an ideal. And you were, sadly, an aberration: a mistake to be avoided. Your whole life would be measured by it. If you failed, like we poor folks did, then the fault was all yours.

III

The model student had a little affair. No one knew. She kept it a secret, and she was quite successful. If any teacher had found out that she was dating a boy, her reputation would have suffered. My friend told me about this love affair. This tale is about them.

Roxanna's beloved was also a lawyer, but he was not from our college. The boy had little talent for law, but he did well enough to pass his semesters with decent scores. He was also a talented singer. The couple went around for two years during which the model student never allowed fucking. Kissing allowed. Hugging allowed. Blowjobs allowed. Fucking was prohibited before marriage.

For two years then, this couple dated in great secrecy. They visited cyber cafes, parks, hotels, dargahs of Sufi saints. They held each other's hand and walked like a model couple.

After this two-year period of courtship, their marriage was solemnized in the presence of people whose faces were painted. Men were hired to dress like chickens, or characters from cartoon TV shows, and entertain the children who flocked around them.

It was the kind of marriage you get to see on Pakistani TV soap operas where even the servants speak impeccable Urdu and English.

IV

Roxanna's husband was really a decent boy. He dutifully took care of his wife. Every weekend he took his wife to watch a movie. And he made love to her afterwards. He worked out almost every day at the gym. He gave up drinking and smoking. He became an ideal husband for her. She rarely found him scolding her. For the next year the couple lived happily. They ate in silence, prayed in silence and made love in silence. And yes, at nights he would sing or hum for Roxanna some of the most soulful songs he had composed. There were moments when Roxanna would sit and think about how happy and lucky she was. Her husband was her lucky charm. She would get up and walk towards him and kiss his forehead. She had never imagined that her life could be this peaceful and beautiful. When she looked outside the window, she saw butterflies. Her world was complete. She thanked the Creator for so much happiness. If happiness is real wealth, then I am the richest person on this planet.

V

One day the husband came back while Roxanna was sitting and reading *The Filmfare*. She could see from a distance that he was exceedingly gay. What is he so happy about? A smile spread over her beautiful face.

"You know, today I bagged a new contract," he said.

"Oh wow! Yeah! Party. That calls for a party."

"It's not related to the law firm," he responded.

"Then."

"I am going to be a singer. I am going to rock and roll baby," he said while playing an imaginary guitar.

He had uploaded a video on YouTube. Some music director had found it. He had liked this new guy. His gruff voice had attracted him. He compared him to Bryan Adams.

The song was recorded in a studio in south Kolkata. It was widely appreciated. Roxanna's husband was popular at last. He had been invited for talk shows on TV and radio. An English daily had even done a story on him. The story of his model life was served with eggs and coffee even to toddlers in the hope that they would grow up and...

Roxanna's life, in short, had become a model life. It had acquired the quality of an object that is kept in a museum for pure reflection.

Soon after this, they left on a vacation. They traveled to Kurseong. It was here that the trouble began. Actually, few people knew about this. People from our college said nothing beyond this. But my friend was ingenious. He had found out every small detail, as if he were writing a novel based on the couple's life.

Roxanna's husband had performed that night in Kurseong. It was quite a successful show. After the show was over, he came out. The air was cool and refreshing. As he walked towards the hotel, he saw the lights shimmer on the opposite mountain. He was dazzled by its sheer beauty and size. The sky that night gave birth to all sorts of constellations. The stars twinkled like big diamonds. He felt as if he had just to raise his hands, and he could shuffle the constellations and play with the stars.

The silence of the night was punctuated by the shrill barks of the emaciated street dogs.

As he lit his first cigar, his thoughts flew towards Roxanna who must be waiting for him. She could never sleep unless he was with her. A strong animal-like desire to caress Roxanna came over him.

As he hurried toward the hotel, he met a boy. His name was Vivek. He was a guitarist who played exceedingly well. He was waiting to see Roxanna's husband. He said that he had to wait for him for three hours, and now in the dead of the night he would have to walk back three miles. He just wanted to play for him. Did he have the time? Roxanna's husband reluctantly agreed to hear him. He did find the boy to be talented. So he said that he should excuse him now and come and see him in the morning. Ten would be fine. Would it?

The meeting was confirmed.

He left the place as soon as he could and, accompanied by his shadow, he returned to his hotel room.

Roxanna woke up quite early in the morning. She left alone to go shopping. Roxanna was back by twelve in the afternoon. As soon as she entered, she sniffed like a dog. Someone had been here, probably a man. When her husband came out of the bathroom, she walked straight to him. She did not even have to smell her husband's chest. She was dead sure of it. Her intuition turned into certainty when she found a used condom in the bathroom. They had thus far not used a condom while making love. As she sat down at the bed with a feeling of thud in her chest, a young boy arrived. Someone had ordered a packet of cigarette and he had come with it. But who had ordered it? Roxanna took the boy aside and asked him. The other man who was here, he confessed without hesitating. He looked like someone from the Hills.

Now, if I were a filmmaker I would not use any dialogue in this scene. I would take the camera and place it right outside the wide French window of the hotel. Her husband would be seen begging, pleading and crying like a sincere actor whose tears move the audience even though they can't really hear him because the window remains shut. Roxanna could be seen gesticulating like a mad woman. The camera would slowly zoom out. The window would grow progressively smaller, one window of Roxanna's room would be replaced by dozens of them. Rows of houses with corrugated roofs, streets with sad yellow lights, children, street dogs and mad men would appear. A soft drizzle would fall, and a sad waltz would play in the background.

By evening, a permanent night had descended upon the life of Roxanna and her ex-husband.

VI

The very next night Roxanna's husband had a strange dream. He saw it as if one were seeing an animated movie in black and white. In the dream he saw one big ship. He saw that he was slowly drifting away from it. There was something he was holding onto, perhaps a small plank of wood. The strength of the waves carried him swiftly. When he turned back, he noticed that the ship was burning. He could see the water burning. For a brief while he saw everything from a great height: the massive ship of fire burned right before his eyes. Even in his dream the mere spectacle made him sick. That was just when he woke up. His throat was dry. He began the day or night if you prefer, with a big glass of rum: Old Monk with water.

Three days after this incident, Roxanna's husband slit his throat open. As blood oozed from his throat, he could feel that he was getting progressively weaker. He could see that he was disintegrating. Part by part, his body was getting heavier and colder. The blood kept oozing, he got weaker and weaker, his vision blurred, his heart beat faster than he had expected. Death made him nervous. He closed his eyes for the last time, not realizing that it was the last time, and his waking mind slipped and fell into a dark and inexplicable hole. For a brief while he felt that he was out in a cloud, looking at the sky like he used to do as a child, then suddenly there was a blinding light, the kind they actually show in sci-fi films. Just then, he died with a vague smile on his face.

The policemen who saw it lost their appetite for food and life for months. It was really horrible. He must have taken at least half an hour to die. Imagine! Half an hour with a slit throat must be really painful. There was so much of blood in the bathroom that the scavengers had to use three bottles of phenol to cleanse the dried blood. The pipe of the bathroom opened onto the drain that carried slaughtered sheep's blood.

After six months, Roxanna came back to Kurseong. For the past few months she had hardly found time to relax. She would wake up and run to court and come back late at night. It is said that she met another man. His name is Vivek. She finds the guy to be really decent. And he is an excellent musician. And she could never love any man who is not an artist.

The day my friend narrated this story to me, that day was Roxanna's first marriage anniversary.

An Extramarital Love Affair

The Story of the Poor Husband

I DON'T know if talent is a thing one receives from heaven or if it is a virtue crafted and acquired day by day, inch by inch. Whatever the case may be, I too, like countless people, possess something called talent. My talent consists in taking inordinate pleasure out of sex. I am crazy about sex. I have found out that there is even a dictionary word for me: nymphomaniac. I simply cannot imagine how people live without it. In the Indian subcontinent, there are millions of ascetics who renounce sex, embrace celibacy and live quietly. I fail to understand this. Anyhow, leaving other things aside, let me compose for you the real tale of my own sexual exploits.

I must inform you that I am a married man. I hate politics. I have a decent job. I live an ordinary life: meaning that my marriage has not yet come to symbolize deep cracks in walls. I have a perfect digitalized wife, the kind that you get to see on TV. She is extraordinarily good looking. When we make love I often find myself observing the following proposition: I find that I am usually caught between my desire to come out, and the desire not to come out. I oscillate nervously in this strange dialectics of sexuality. If I come out the game is over. But if I don't, then the desire to release my energy troubles me.

Thesis is the desire to come out. Antithesis is the desire not to come out. Synthesis, the unreal real state of being, the moment of ejaculation, is the state where contradictions embrace one another.

When I spoke about this to a fellow lawyer at the firm, he suggested that I eat dates. He thought that I was suffering from some sexual problem. But I know that you know exactly what I am talking about.

Lawyers are stupendously dumb. I always knew this, but this colleague merely provided me yet another piece of oral evidence.

One day, it was raining. The rain fell from the sky like an army of needles. The narrow alleys of our city came to resemble a complicated network of rivers filled with black ink. The untreated industrial effluent made it worse. It smelled of tablets. Street dogs were stupidly swimming.

I have a good old friend who is an engineer. We are fond of each other; much to my wife's discomfiture. She hates him. So, that day I arrived at his home. His younger brother appeared before the gate. His head was tilted to the right so that he could hold his cell-phone on his shoulder pressed against his ears. With a mug of rum we sat. It was raining outside. The trees were swaying their branches. Like us they were enjoying the cool rain.

Just then my smart engineer friend received a call. 'Shreetoma.' My friend got up and disappeared. His shadow appeared on the wall of the next room after some twenty minutes. He was speaking to her and settling his unruffled hair.

So, he arrived out of the blue and demanded that I make a Patiala peg for him. "Make it a big one," he said.

"How many *Patialas* can you endure?" I asked.

"Maybe six," he said after a long pause.

"I won't be able to withstand two," I quipped.

"This is why I told you not to get married. Marriage kills the demon in you. Get this bitch."

We laughed like drunken poets who live their drunken truths.

It was late in the night. We were both pretty drunk. I could see one object, let us say a spoon, multiply in three. You can very well understand my condition.

We walked out into the terrace. The sky had cleared. The stars twinkled like millions of diamond pendants. At one go, we both saw three shooting stars. The honking of cars had subsided; it had retreated back to their motor, back to the battery, back to the oil tank.

My friend now lighted a cigarette. As he inhaled it the red ash brightened. And then slowly it grew faint. Bright. Faint. Bright. Faint. Then he passed it to me. I found out that day that if you drink too much, you simply can't have sex. You can only *imagine* it. So we started to discuss the thing we love most: sex.

My friend is a weirdo. He never fucks the same woman more than once.

"I don't like repetitions," he would say like a serious man of the world.

Egged on by the rum we sat there for three hours. Later, I could hardly recall what else we had discussed. Life is like this. You remember, you forget, you remember to remember and forget that you have forgotten.

We both decided to go to bed. At about four-thirty in the morning I woke up. I could feel and hear the vibration of my friend's cell-phone. I saw myself that I was taking the phone. My consciousness was like that lamp that crackles, tries to come alive when it is lighted. My being, I supposed, was oscillating between dream and faint wakefulness.

I finally woke up. I then realized that it was in the dream that I had picked up the phone. It was there right before me shaking like a troubled spirit.

"Hello," I said.

An awkward silence.

"This is K, Sengupta's friend. He is currently dead as a stone," I said in English.

"May I know who this is?" I further asked.

"I am his friend. Okay. Tell him when he wakes up that I called him."

I disconnected the phone. Later I paused to wonder who that girl was. How did she look? Her voice was so sonorous. How old is she? Seventeen?

I laid on the bed. My heart was troubling me.

Out of an urge, I took my phone, found her number from Sengupta's cell phone and send her a SMS: "I am sorry if I sounded a bit rude to you. We had a party. And we drank like fish."

The next morning I saw the reply: "It is okay."

My heart shrunk like a balloon. She had shown no interest in me. Did she know how good looking a man I was? No. Perhaps not.

I had forgotten all about this. The fragment of memory laid hidden like a chit in the dusty attic of my mind. It was quite late in the night. I was working on my case related to custodial deaths. I received a phone call.

"May I speak to Sengupta," said the voice.

"Who?"

"Sengupta."

"Ah, no. It is not Sengupta's number. This is his lawyer-friend's number. If you want, I could give you his number," I said sincerely.

"But then how did you get my number," I further asked.

Silence.

"Actually you had sent me a text that day," she responded.

Just then the dust of present that had accumulated on the chit of the past cleared. The whole of the past rolled before my mind like a trailer of a movie I had seen not very long ago. The phone call, the text message.

I grew excited. My dead flirtatious brain cells resurrected. I understood that the girl was trying to initiate a conversation. I controlled the street dog in me and informed her that right now I am busy. Could I call her after eleven thirty?

"Is that okay!"

"Yes," she said.

By eleven my wife slept. On the dot at eleven thirty I called her. After an hour's conversation I found out that she was not a girl, a Lolita of sorts, as I had imagined. She was an unmarried woman roughly of Anna Karenina's age.

We had such a hot conversation that, were I to write it here, word by word, sentence by sentence, idea by idea, then I would be kicked right in my teeth by the guardians of morality.

I could summarize the whole conversation in these few words. She kept complaining that she was not that beautiful. Several men had deserted her. And yes, she preferred sex both ways. When I heard this, my whole body was on fire.

I don't remember when I had suffered so much. Peeping back into that night I realize what a strange creature a man is. Like a shopaholic he is constantly on a mission to seek, to collect, to possess. And he keeps doing it. He keeps repeating it, until the dots of memory that comprise the enterprise of existence are cut short by death. The thought of her kept pursuing me. And the fact that I had not even seen her made it all the worse. How trying it is for a soul to be tormented by a face he has not seen. I realized the meaning of this simple truth that night.

I spent the night overcome with fever. I kept imagining all sorts of things that I was doing to her. The night passed slowly as in a fixated dream. Time stood still on the folds of the windowpanes. Time was the still windowpane, the pillow, the chairs, the band of moonlight on the floor of my room.

I kept rolling my body from one side of the bed to the other. I don't remember exactly when my hyperactive consciousness fell into a void, but like the screen of a TV, it abruptly shut down. The forest of images running in the universe of my mind became a small dot. Then all was dark.

The Story of the Poor Wife

My husband is my part-time husband and a full time drunkard. He always drinks and then says strange things. He says that a man never dies. He merely changes his form. Today, say he is all bone and flesh; tomorrow he may be a fossil or grass. Men die, human civilizations perish, imperial cities rise and fall, but man, he says, is immortal. When a man is born, he is torn away from nature. He tries to understand this mystery. He miserably fails. That is why he is always at war with nature: always fighting, always destroying it. Once he dies, once he changes his form, he participates in the process of regeneration of biological life. Man is *Brahma* (the creator), man is *Vishnu* (the sustainer) and man is *Shiva* (the annihilator). Man he says *is* God. He says these things with such intellectual gusto that I am often aghast. He is always so sure of himself, I think. How foolish these young people are! I married my husband out of pure whim. I thought he had such kissable lips and a decent job: for me this was enough.

Some three months ago, we visited a beach. It was so quiet and peaceful. The days were warm, and dogs ran on the beach. When my husband saw it, he said look, there are two dogs there. Two, I asked. But I can only see one. There is one on the mud, see it properly. You can only see the yellow one; see, there is a black one as well pasted on the wet beach. As the dog ran, so did his reflection on the wet beach. He laughed. I laughed. We laughed.

Later, my husband left me alone in the room. He always does that to me. I think he likes taking revenge. His sweet little matrimonial revenge! All husbands are like that: cruel and inconsiderate toward their wives. I lay on the bed to watch TV. I mean one of those movies with a disturbing socio-religious subtext: Muslims are not terrorist type film. Okay I get it. Now bug off. I then watched a sleazy Bollywood film, which was full of cheap sexual innuendoes. I didn't mind. Sex kills boredom, my poor husband often says. He is not wrong as I see it.

You should have seen my husband's eyes when he came back. They were red as a sliced pomegranate. Had his mother seen him in this condition, how would she have reacted to it, I kept thinking. When I said this to him, he screamed back that he was not a kid anymore. He could well take care of himself and blah and blah. Men are so stupid. They just don't get anything. Talk to them about sky and stars, they will wonder at your wisdom, and just show them the well near their feet and they will scream. My father was exactly like him. But I have no qualms against him. It is okay. He is better than most men.

The same night I saw in my dream that my husband was lying dead on the beach. Rising waves sucked his body. And then he appeared once again in the distant cliff. This time a vulture was circling his corpse. I awoke with a feeling of intense guilt. It was as if I had myself killed him. In the past I had seen my mother, my younger sister dead. This one was different. The sense of guilt was overwhelming. The worst part was that I could not talk about this to anyone. They would think that I was really mad.

The next morning my husband asked me to accompany him to the beach. I did. He sat, as usual, drinking beer after beer. I felt intensely bored. After a while, a crowd had gathered near the waves. I could see a white screen that is used during the shooting of films. I got up and walked toward it. I could almost feel my husband's eyes on my shoulder. The director said: rolling, action and then the girl and boy started splashing water. The heroine's cheeks were red as cherry. Her waterproof make up made her glow in the heat of the beach.

"Cut, cut, cut," the director shouted.

"Is this how you throw water?"

The hero protested. The director's voice rose. He got so impatient that he threw the butt of cigarette near his feet, which was already sunk in ankle-deep water. Then he tried to crush it. See, I thought, how foolish men are. I felt like laughing. But I kept quiet. My husband soon arrived. He took hold of my hand and asked me if I would take a toto ride. The toto driver promised to show us red crabs. We agreed like children going to a picnic.

Even today I can picture the ride. After ten minutes or so, the salt-white beach was spotted with red crabs. They seemed to move in unison like an army. On hearing any kind of noise they'd disappear into the sand. The beach was wide and open. I had never seen anything so serene in my life. I was terrified by the idea that I stood at the very end of human civilization. The beach had come to an end. There was land on the other side of a small tributary. As my eyes surveyed the horizon of the ocean, I was overcome with a sense of acute poetic melancholia that I still cannot describe in words. I saw my husband speak to the driver. He was so friendly with him, as if the man was his childhood friend. My husband is like this: when he gets drunk he becomes jolly and garrulous. Otherwise, he stays locked in his own shell. He was in one of his happy moods.

The two hours that I had spent in the company of red crabs and my husband, who stood at a distance, as he often does when I see him in my dreams, appear like an illusion to me now. Like icebergs, they are already melting, and I, who lived them, can do nothing about it. There is no court of memory where my husband could go and file a case to reclaim our past. There is no bureaucratic office where my husband could bribe someone and get the past back to us, the past as we lived it.

My husband soon appeared and said, "The man says there is a village on the other side of the tributary. He can take us there."

"We have to go back," I reminded him.

He fell silent.

As we returned, I could feel a pinch of sand on my teeth. The air smelled of raw fish that had just emerged from the bowels of the ocean. Fishermen carrying their nets appeared as they often do in an Ernest Hemmingway novel. A group of elderly women with melancholic faces sat at the same spot where I had seen them in the afternoon. Someday I too will grow like them, I thought. The beach was full of couples who fondled each other under the spell of chilled beer and marijuana. They populated the relatively empty spots. How unromantic my husband was, I realized that day.

As we entered our beautiful, Disney-inspired brightly colored villa, I noticed the footprints we had made as we walked from the beach. Dots of footprints, one trailing behind another appeared on the beach, like the prints of a tiger's paw. They had begun at the point in the beach where we stepped down from the toto and ended at my feet. Our past laid trapped in those footprints, and it would stay there so long as the waves did not hit them. My husband said back then that this is life. Nothing survives: neither literature nor man. Both are doomed. What a gloomy thing to say! Everything is falling into darkness, the sun is burning out leaving dark ashes in its wake, and blackest clouds stacked up in the sky. There is no hope of sunshine, of rain and life. And the circle of absurdity of human existence comes full. Why does he harbor such dark thoughts?

I stood there and thought for a long while. How cute my husband appears when he gets drunk and playacts the perfect bookish philosophe. I came back and ate my dinner. Then I watched TV while he sat reading some novel I think.

The Story of the Poor Mistress

The evening when I first saw him I was astounded. I could see that not very long ago he was a teenager. The traces of his teenage lingered on his chiseled face. He was twenty-eight and I was thirty-five (actually forty-five). He was so innocent that he could not guess that I had lied about my age. I often lie and quite enjoy it at times. He also did not know that I was a married woman.

My husband lived not very far from the kitchen where we made our maiden love. He had lived there until a few months ago. My husband had fucked my younger sister. Then he proceeded to screw my twin cousins. And then that son of bitch fucked his maid. That is when I said, enough is enough. I exploded and organized a boycott movement against him. He later even spoke to me about this mess. He confessed that deep in heart, he desired to fuck "everyone with a pair of boobs." I decided then and there that this madman must be kicked out from our locality.

At first I had thought that K was like other men who don't have any idea that they don't have any idea about anything whatsoever. I had thought that we'd make love, eat, speak about mundane things – that's all. But with him it was different. There was so much we could talk about. Unlike my husband, who was absent even when he was present, K was present even during his long absences. His small-small thoughts on a wide variety of subjects floated around my head like words entrapped within bubbles, as in a comic strip.

Day after day, we met at one of those hotel rooms that are dark even during the day. The smell of Bengal naphthalene balls emanating from the all-white bed still brings tears of joy to my eyes. How happy we were then, drinking port wine, making love like wild boars and reading old Russian novels of Turgenev that he'd bring from College Street.

I cannot mention the name of the hotel where all this transpired. But I can give you the room number. It was 103. Our happiest hours were those when we read to each other novels, cheap gossip magazines, newspapers, F.I.R's, articles and essays about writers virtually unknown to me. Golden rays of light fell onto the pages, as we raced through the tales of love, death and agony.

Night would fall and then we'd part with tearful eyes. How I had come to love him. It wasn't like the way I parted with my husband or boss from the office – with a sense of relief. I had genuinely come to love him.

Notes of the Poor Husband

That evening when my wife stood at the outer bounds of the hotel studying our footprints, I was inside the bathroom. I had contracted a nausea. It was a slight one, and it left me without much trouble. I lay on my bed. Then I did what I usually do. I closed my eyes and imagined that I was walking toward my wife. I regularly play this sort of game. When I was a child, I would close my eyes and imagine like this that I was taking an imaginary walk to meet my grandma at her house. Sometimes, I would take my older sister with me. We both would close our eyes, then I would say, so we leave our home, get out of the door, and see the dogs. Now we have reached the meat shop. My sister would reply, no wait I am still standing near the tea stall.

My wife and I left the next morning. As the car sped, the villages of Bengal stood painted before our eyes. The endless fields were ripe with rice and coconut.

When I see these utopian villages before me, I feel weak. I feel like getting out of the car, building a home here, and saying a final big no to this fucked up world.

As the car sped on, these thoughts crossed my mind, and as usual I found my ego standing at the crossroads of my thoughts and laughing at me. They soon dissolved into the air like the smoke of a burning cigarette.

The car passed by identical looking villages filled with ponds of more or less the same shape. Buffaloes chewed their grass with no care or notion of time; they weren't in a hurry.

As we boarded the train I sat on the leeward side of the window. Villages painted in green appeared endlessly. I shut my eyes. The screen of my mind was a perfect luminous orange. Just then I could hear the roar of the approaching train. I saw the cargo train pass. I shut my eyes again. Now the orange of my mind was interspersed with boxes of black. I opened my eyes. I could make out that it became orange only when the sun could hit my eyes for the brief whiles when the compartment separated and allowed the sun. Orange... black... orange... black.... Then it was once again infinite orange.

How the next three months of my life went by, I don't know. It was pretty quick. I did the same things, at more or less the same time, with more or less the same thoughts revolving in my mind. How strange that I never paused to think about this back then.

When I reached my office I was always in a hurry to rush back to my home. And once I reached my home, its serenity troubled me. I was left with nothing much to do.

When I walked the dusty streets of the north, populated with old homes, where trees carelessly grow on the walls, I'd think that my real being, my real self was walking ahead of me. I was following it; I was pursuing it without any hope of ever meeting myself. My real self was like that friend with whom I was trapped in a revolving door. He was ahead of me, always, and I was following him.

One such evening I was sitting at the Tollygunge Metro station. I was all set to go meet my mistress. I received a call from my wife's phone. She had fallen on the floor, she was bleeding, and she needed urgent medical care. My father, who spoke to me, asked me to come back urgently.

"You are always missing from home when we need you the most," he said to me.

I decided to cancel my rendezvous and rush back to my wife. As I stood at the counter to buy my ticket, I received another call. This was one from my so-called mistress. Her neighbor, who spoke, informed me too that my mistress had fallen, and she was bleeding. They asked me if I could come and take her to the hospital.

Thus I stood, on an ordinary evening at the Tollygunge Metro Station trapped between two lives. Ask me now the meaning of the fable of Abraham's anguish, and I could tell you a tale or two.

The Perforated Bed Sheet

THE DAYS were bright. The air was fresh and refreshing. Birds chirped all day long in the dense forest of Kurseong. The dark-green pines, tall as a waterfall, stood eternal. The warm rays of the morning sun pierced the branches of the pines and fell obliquely on the chimney of the house. The clear stream of water appeared like molten diamond. The forest was washed with pearl-shaped droplets of water. She walked towards the bush, collected a pearl of dew on the tip of her finger and examined it under the rays of sun like a scientist. This young girl, the heroine of our story had just arrived at the hill station. She had just encountered a tragic incident that had sucked all the juice of life from her soul. She wanted to see no one and be seen by no one.

This story began one afternoon when she boarded the train. There are moments, those isolated atoms of memory, that remain stuck in our mind. It was one such moment. She stood at the station with a book in her hand, and she found immense consolation in merely holding it. In the past three days, she had walked the streets with the book, holding it tightly despite the sweat

in her hand. She had merely read ten or twelve pages. But
in those three days she had come to like the smell of the
pages, the light yellow hardbound cover and the zigzag
patterned print of the book. She felt that a part of her
soul was trapped inside it.

She boarded the train and sat quietly, gazing absentmindedly outside the window. Once the train left, the
electric wire and the parallel tracks of train started to
move with her. As a child she had once secretly announced this to her mother, who had kissed her on her
forehead and said, *pagal* (lunatic), out of motherly affec-
tion. She remembered all this. The glass widow pane,
which was pulled down, displayed the tranquil rural life of
north India. The fields were vast and endlessly open like
an ocean. Once in a while, as the train moved, her vulture
eyes could see the chocolate brown skinned children
throwing off their half pants before they would splash
their bodies in the village pond where buffaloes stood in
neck-deep water.

She studied these images patiently, like a painter, and
regretted the idea that she had thus far not taught herself
the art of painting. Having absorbed these images she
shut her eyes and tried hard to imagine them in the screen
of her mind. She realized that she was unable to do so.
The images vanished, the more she tried. It was melting
like a slab of ice. It had already melted. She sat there
pondering over the fact that if the images from one's
memory slowly disappear, then what will be the fate of
the mind that stores these images?

An extremely good-looking boy arrived to take his seat
opposite her. The train had stopped at Aligarh Station.
He was a student, as she found out. The young man, it
appeared, was well read. He was writing his dissertation
on Michel Foucault. At first, the girl did not bother to

look at him. And moreover, this boy was not a typical talkative modern man. He preferred to converse with himself. It was both a habit and a deep human, all too human, need. The train blew its whistle. She saw the train opposite her moving; but within few seconds she realized it was her train. No, that train is moving! No, this train is moving!

It was just then that the young man interrupted her and said, "Don't worry, this is the train that is moving, not that."

She looked back at him with a sense of disbelief. How did you know, she wanted to ask him. But she did not.

The train moved, hawkers arrived, passengers left and the journey continued. It was late in the night, when she decided to go to sleep. She took out her bed sheet and spread it over the seat. The young man now sat on the top seat. But it appeared that he had nothing to cover his body. The wind was chilled enough to give electric shocks to young and old alike. She thought for a while and then took out an extra, perforated, bed sheet and handed it to the boy. He was shy and he refused it. But she persisted. And he consented.

The next morning when she woke up she found that the boy had left. He had probably got down at some station. But he had left behind a book with a note in it. She read her love letter in his beautiful handwriting. Thus began her third and his first love affair. This continued for the next three months. The day she arrived at her home, she sat down at her table. She stayed there, with her right hand placed now under her chin, now on the table. She was learning, like a bird, to sing the same old tunes of love that had overcome her. In short, she had, thanks mainly to the notes, and the book, and the boys' extremely sweet looks, fallen head over heels in love with him. She had written almost half the letter when she realized that she was merely repeating herself. I had said, more or less the same things even to him. This realization made her freeze in a moment of reflection. But she continued to write the letter. She finished it with an appropriate love song that she had recently heard. Thus their love grew, out of distance. It kept growing, allowing each in the solemn comforts of a private world to imagine the other.

They had exchanged, like neurotic characters from Spanish novellas, some two trunks of letters. But this ended abruptly like a rainfall in summer. For a period of two months she did not receive any letter. She grew restless and finally decided to visit the boy. She took a train and arrived at Howrah Station whose busyness had always made him marvel at the wonder of human civilization. How it flourished, despite all the dirt and filth. She took, on purpose, the steamer services. How beautifully he had described the landscape of the city, as seen through a moving steamer: the Ghats where men shaved their hairs and where young boys sat in groups under the shadow of century-old trees to smoke marijuana. She noticed, like him, the long rows of plastic-made huts, the pigs, the rag pickers of the city who picked each other's lice.

She finally reached his home. His mother opened the gate and looked into her eyes like a sick, aging woman who until yesterday looked young, hale and hearty. It was through his mother that she found out that the boy had died in a bomb blast. The bed sheet she had given him was spread on the bed where he had once slept. The girl wept. His mother wept. And the white cat that sat on the red mat got up and left the room.

Two Friends

"*ABE CHUTIYA* (oye asshole), what are you up to?" said Salim.

"Nothing much. I was just playing games on my cell phone," replied Pintu.

Salim and Pintu were best of friends. Theirs was a friendship of brick and cement.

"So what's your plan?"

"Plan. Plan for what?"

"For tonight, *Meri jaan* (My beloved)."

"I have no plan whatsoever," said Pintu.

"Then let's go there!"

"Where?"

"To the sin city, my beloved. You take one. I will pluck a new cherry for myself."

"But I don't have much money."

"It's okay. I'll lend you some. Repay me later. Let's go man. Please, I am dying to fuck someone."

Thus Salim and Pintu decided to visit the brothel located at Sonargachi. I am sure you must have seen the black walls of those brothels where whores line up, walk, chat, eat *pani-puri*, paint lipsticks and punch their cell phones on the footpath leading up to Mahatma Gandhi Road.

They met at six in the evening.

II

Some seven years ago Salim had, in a heat of passionate longing, asked Pintu to come and join him at Jayshree Cinema Hall. It is now extinct. Back in those days, at specified hours, rickshaw pullers, *bidi*-makers, jute mill workers, unemployed youths and groups of veteran old men with shiny bald heads would congregate. The final bell would fill the air, men would grow talkative and then one by one they would enter the dark hall that smelled of whiskey and *ghutkas*. These men would sit and watch wonders of sexual tales unfold before their eyes.

It was Friday. Salim had just offered his afternoon prayer with sweat dripping from his armpit. He had received intelligence that they were showing *French Kamasutra*. The hall was unusually packed. Suddenly, young Muslim men had emerged from nowhere. They were selling black-market tickets.

"*Ek da bis, ek ka bis*" (one for twenty, one for twenty), they kept shouting.

Those days, I must tell you, anything European enjoyed, as it does even now, a godly air, and this one had *Kamasutra* as well. It was doubly lucrative.

During the intermission, Salim came out on the terrace, which was filled with the stench of urine. When Salim walked to pee, he saw an old man who, like him, was relieving himself. Salim felt that the man was lovingly staring at his penis. He felt anger and humiliation rise in him. The old man left. Salim now turned to his right. He saw a shopkeeper who lived near his home.

Salim saw the shopkeeper seeing him. The shopkeeper saw that he was seeing Salim seeing him. Salim immediately left the terrace and located Pintu. He took him out and narrated the scene – I mean the shopkeeper one, not the penis staring one.

Pintu laughed like a lunatic. "Don't worry, he won't go and sneak it to anybody."

Later, as both boys walked the street with their slightly wet underwear, Salim could not help but imagine a world of easy and relaxed morals norms. It was likewise no surprise that months later they would both find themselves in grip of whores.

III

I don't know how it happened, but Salim felt in love with a whore. I don't know if this is also true, but in the world of whoring, it is said that whores don't fall for anyone, and when they do, they go crazy. One day, Salim, then still a high-school student, had just entered the brothels that are busy as beehives.

As he walked the wooden stairs guided by the pimp, girls giggled at him.

"Are Shahrukh Khan aya hai" (Shahrukh Khan has come).

Every room was partitioned by curtains. There were big beds as well. They too were partitioned into two and three. He found out that those ten-by-ten rooms were actually places where, at one go, five men fucked five whores. This sociological discovery struck him. Imagine one man moaning umm… umm… and his immediate neighbour saying uhh… uhhh….

The pimp, who was a physically disabled boy kept telling the whores to mind their business. He told Salim that his fruit is upstairs.

When Salim finally reached the top floor he saw a group of girls standing. On his left side he saw a one-eyed whore. She was fat. But trust me, she was beautiful. Her breasts were perfectly round. Salim had seen her the last time as well.

"I want this one," he said pointing the finger to her.

The whore smiled. He was her first client for the day.

"*Aye Champa Uth*" (Champa get up).

Among the wise it is said that those hours that Salim spent with Champa were enough to shake his bowels. She had drained the lust out of him. He emerged from her room bathed in the freshness of her soul. As he stood in the queues for an auto, he could still smell her skin on his hands, upper lips and even his chest.

So Salim arrived at the same brothel with Pintu. This happened a day or two later. Sadly, he could not find Champa, his elephantine whore carved out of fat and flesh. She had gone to her *muluk* (home town).

Babu, why don't you pick out one from here, said the pimp who was drinking his beer from a transparent plastic glass. Their aunty was sitting at the wooden stool. When Salim noticed her, she was busy taking out betel leaf from her silver box and placing it between her teeth. Her hair had been dyed in red. She appeared exactly as the aunts whom one sees in classic Hindi cinema.

The girls he saw did not impress him at all. He could make out that their belly bore pregnancy marks.

Just then Salim saw a sad looking whore who was staring below. Salim walked towards her. She remained unmoved. Perhaps she did not even feel his presence. Salim was now leaning on the faded dark green wooden balcony. Below the balcony the man selling kebabs was doing hectic business.

The tram appeared. It stopped. It hissed. A group of office going elderly men and school children with white ribbons got down. And it moved. As usual, men jostled one another to get a glimpse of their mistress of fantasy who appeared before the windows humming the latest Bollywood songs.

The melancholic whore whose fictional name is Sapna (Dream) smiled at Salim. He had never seen someone so beautiful *this* sad. He held her hands and later smoked a joint. He turned back to Pintu who was as usual busy teasing girls and giving them lively company.

"Pintu, this is your *Bhabi* (sister-in-law)." The girls laughed in unison. Someone burst out saying *Oh Ma*.

Because Sapna was actually a dream, a Sapna, she did everything for Salim. Salim in turn would never forget to tip her more money than she charged. I think it was there, under the guidance and consortship of Sapna, that he first learned what magic laid hidden in his own body. It was she who taught him to explore the vast, almost impenetrable, regions of his soul. It was she who helped him to discover that lightening region of his being where he ceased to exist as I, or he or thou. The deeper you go into yourself, the deeper shall you be in me, she would tell Salim as he put on his rugged denim jeans.

When he walked the street with Pintu, Salim said to him that Sapna was not just a whore, she also had a talent for poetry. Pintu smiled and got busy with his cell phone.

IV

One day both Salim and Pintu appeared before their Hindi teacher. Like all Hindi teachers' homes, it was nearly empty and squalid. The man, Mr. P. Singh, was extremely courteous. He was not effeminate; nor did he display the aggressive manliness so typical of those who teach natural science or physical education. The man it seemed, because of his intense devotion to books on history, philosophy, political economy, painting, literature and cinema, was able to negotiate a space between the two distinct binary modes of being in the world.

Both boys were profoundly in awe of the man. Unlike others, to begin with, Mr. Singh did not feel scandalized whenever he found out that one of his students was watching the soft-porn pictures that regularly appear in magazines. On the contrary he encouraged them.

"Sex education is quite liberating, if you can use it to that end," he used to say.

And his words echoed in the near-empty minds of his pupils.

V

Salim entered the mosque. He was to offer his prayer, and after the 4:40 evening prayer he had promised to Pintu that they both would go watch a B-grade porn film: *shaadi ke baad* (After the Marriage). Salim was tormented by the pornographic images that he had stocked up in the library of his mind. "Oh God please forgive me. Please. I didn't do it intentionally. God please. God I am sorry. I deserve to be punished. Please give me one last chance. Please God. Please don't pour molten oil on my skin. Don't roast me alive. Please God, the Satan has taken hold of my soul," thus Salim finished his tormented prayer one evening.

Later, when Salim confessed this to Pintu, he said that the same thing happened to him as well when he stood before the Gods to prayer. *Madar-Swear, Madar-swear,* he kept repeating to himself while softly pinching his Adam's apple with his left hand.

Thus their guilt cancelled one another, and their life went on as usual. Their final high-school exam was due to begin in March.

After the exam was over, Pintu, on a whim, suggested that they go out of the city for a short vacation. Money and parental consent were arranged as soon as they could. Then they arrived at Sealdah Railway Station.

The train was scheduled to leave at nine. Both boys were in a drunken state. Their eyes revealed the gallons of whiskey that had been stored in the pit of their stomachs.

In the main gate, the scene was the usual. Hundreds of men, women and children painted in black were sitting or lying on their cots placed in a long rows.

Next to the main gate, two small mountains of yellow sand had been kept. A dog appeared from nowhere. He climbed the summit and sat like a lion. A dirty naked child arrived. It was a girl, and she was running toward the sand mountain. She climbed it and sat on the dog. She took hold of the ears of the dog and began taking an imaginary ride.

When Salim saw this, he laughed. He turned back to see where Pintu was, and what he saw scared him. Pintu was being beaten by a group of vendors. He had probably misbehaved with one of them. Salim intervened. By then a purple circle had been punched on Pintu's right eye.

They decided to cancel the visit. From that day, Pintu bore a secret hostility against Salim. He felt that, had Salim intervened on time, that son of a bitch, *chai-walla* (tea vendor) would not have painted my eye.

"Hadn't you seen how ugly I looked? I couldn't even see my sweetheart."

On the surface, things remained as they were. The festival of life continued.

Salim came back to his home from Asansol six months later, after cracking his entrance exam by sheer luck and gaining admission to an engineering college. When he came home for the first time, he rushed straight to the brothel to meet Sapna.

Pintu always had suspicions regarding Salim's sanity. That afternoon when Salim confessed to him his decision to marry Sapna, his suspicion was satisfied beyond a reasonable doubt. The boy is insane, he kept thinking. How could a man like him even think of marrying a whore? This thought kept him awake in the night.

Now Pintu, because he was Pintu, went straight to Salim's father and sneaked him everything. Salim's father was so scandalized that he called his Hindi teacher for a meeting. This meeting took place at the decided location and the decided time, but it was also the last meeting. Why? This, nobody knows. Anyhow, Salim's left ear was bandaged when he came back to his hostel.

When the boys asked him, he gave such a banal reply that everybody understood he was lying.

"Doctor, I fell in the bathroom," is what he had said to the Doctor who had attended him.

After this, a lot of things happened to the people about whom we have been thinking. Insofar as our Hindi Master is concerned, it has been said that he has actually gone mad. Salim's father's stays all alone with his cat. Pintu lives with a sense of pride: the pride of having taught his friend a good lesson. Actually, on the night when Salim had slit his wrists, Pintu had visited the brothel. He had located Sapna who, shell-shocked, had spent the night with him. Sapna is said to have gone missing after that night. Nobody knows where she is.

First Sorrow

WHEN IRFAN awoke in the morning, it took him a while to recall the horror of the preceding night. At about 1 a.m., in the dead of the night, when his mother found out that he was wide awake, she said, pointing to the window, "baby go the sleep or else the ghost will come and take you away."

Despite the self-attested bravery of a boy of nine, Irfan felt scared. His throat became dry as an empty well. All through the night, as starved dogs barked, an image of a deformed man with rotten teeth and a dirty, stinky and greyish beard hung on the window, or so he imagined. The big, swollen fingers of this ghost clutched the vertical blue bars of the window. The image hung on the window; he imagined the image; he imagined his helpless self imagining the image. A sense of loneliness accentuated his fear. Dots of perspiration, those pearls of childish sweat cropped up on his upper lips and forehead. He had to cover his face under the bed sheet despite the heat, and he felt stultified. It was as if someone had locked him in a hole. His parents slept soundly, lost like Alice in the divine, colorful world of dreams. Everything, all his animal-like fear of the unknown died when the macabre image was replaced by the image of god. He had seen TV and knew what god looked like. His mother, his mermaid *ammi*, had always taught him to say god's name one hundred times whenever he found himself in trouble and alone. The remedy helped. An old man with a white turban had replaced the ghoulish creature. After the tempest of fear had died, he felt lulled.

The compartment of memory of the whole night passed his mind. He sat on a corner of the bed, eyeing his mother who laid asleep with feline languidness. She opened her deer eyes and smiled at him. Slowly, as Irfan was growing up, slowly, he resembled his father. Irfan looked at his mother with a yearning that a churchgoer reserves for the icon of Christ. His mother raised her angelic arms. Irfan moved to her. He kissed her nape. He fondled her arms. He inhaled her Boroline-scented body. He clutched his mother like a money plant clutches a bamboo.

II

Behind his father's palatial house, there was a huge granary of the Food Corporation of India. It was stuffed with grains and snakes. The granary was manned by the aging guards who, in order to lead an honest life, did not mind accepting *haftas* (weekly bribes), as most government officials do. If there was food on one side of the wall, there was Dickensian hunger on the other. Theft was encouraged by everyone: police and public alike. With thieving and hoarding of grains appeared gambling. Those who lived in the *bustee* (neighborhood) were after all those who came from the lowest rung of our marvelously complex society. If our society could be compared with a building with say, one thousand stories in it, then these people would stay either in the underground basement or in the parking lot.

Next to the granary or attached to it was a vast field. So vast, it could actually contain as many as four cargo trains. But, separating this field from the *bustee*, was a wall. Except for thieves, no one dared to climb the wall and risk being shot dead. But once, it so happened that the local people had become fed up with gambling. It was spreading, as everyone acknowledged, like a spider's web. So people organized a crackdown on this ancient game that was known for ruining hundreds of life.

If my memory serves me accurately, then I am reminded of the afternoon when the kingpin of this vice, popularly known as *Mama Shakuni*, the one-eyed gambler, was dragged by his collar along the alley. His hands had been fixed to a bamboo that was tied horizontally to his shoulder. Children with expressions of curiosity on their faces had lined both sides of the dirty alley. *Mama Shakuni's* shirt was sprinkled with the freshest blood. Every now and then, a young muscular boy would pop from the crowd that followed him and beat him with a bamboo stick. Blows rained. Blood dripped from his eyeslashes and nose. Red ants circled the small red dots of blood that were left behind by the crowd as it surged ahead in pursuit of justice. Women who stood by covered their foreheads with *dupatta* and sighed involuntarily. Dogs howled sympathetically, or so it seemed. For a while no one gambled. Then some genius punched a hole in the wall. Now the latent desire for gambling once again flourishes as ever before.

News very soon spread like sunlight, that a hole had been punched in the wall. All the boys, Irfan included, had gathered to decide if they would climb the wall against their parental wishes. Twelve out of thirteen boys voted for the motion. Boredom was prevalent, and the boys knew everything there was to know about sex, so playing cricket seemed an excellent option in a big field. Only Pintu, that is the thirteenth boy, who was referred to as "polio" was against it. He knew he would not be taken with them. In case of raid by the police, he would not be able to run away from government property. But democracy, as you know, has its own internal logic. It does not wait for the wailing minority. So, one afternoon all the boys minus Pintu left their homes.

The moment they reached the wall, they found out why their parents had created such a furor. Just below the hole of the wall, children defecated. The place reeked of shit and tons of urine. Irfan noticed three mountains of yellow shit. Bees, flies, mosquitoes and god knows what not buzzed around it. A dog appeared. A healthy, yellow dog with black spots appeared. It rolled its tongue over it. And by an act of magic, sorry by an act of not-magic, the cakes disappeared.

The boys cried almost in unison: Ehhh, Ehhh, Chee, *Cheeeee!*

Once the field had been discovered or invented, the cricket matches flourished. Unemployed men gambled now openly under the sky while young adolescent boys played their usual India versus Pakistan cricket matches. Soon, as if it was ordained by fate, boys learned how to gamble and men how to play cricket. As if this was not enough, when people slowly realized how gambling sessions had acquired the longevity of classic five-day-long cricket matches, whereas cricket matches now served merely as a prop for betting. The matches continued, the gambling continued, and so did everything else. One

Sunday while clouds travelled over Irfan's head, he entered the ground via the famous hole. Two boys whom he knew followed him. In the distance he could see the guy touted as Waqar Yunis bowling his legendary bouncers. The faces of those who were involved with the game were much tensed. It meant that a big sum was involved in the game. One of the boys who had followed him now came and asked Irfan to come to the other end of the field.

"We need to talk to you," he said.

Irfan, that cow-headed boy followed him. And what happened next was something no one could have reasonably anticipated. Irfan was made to lie on the track of the rail and was forcefully kissed. He could see two devilish faces, one on each side, clearly mimicking villains from soft-porn films, who pouted exaggeratedly at one of those poor women whose eternal status is to be raped in film after film. Their mouths resembled those of a pig. The more he struggled, the more humiliated he felt. The boys were in no mood to let him off. Irfan experienced the topping of the cake moment when the boys who were now behaving like men, said to Irfan that they did that to him, because he looked like Mamta Kulkarni; a sleazy actor who had acquired cult status after having posed naked for a gossip magazine cover. The masculinized man in him who dreamed of joining the army, felt humiliated. And it had to. It was after this incident that Irfan quit going to the Eden Gardens, the word with which he had baptized the place.

It was a typical Friday afternoon in the *bustee*. Pressure cookers were as busy as the engine of a fast moving train, and they were steaming in symphonic harmony. Voices of mothers could be heard shouting; here and there TV was as usual showing the lousy cinema, and children stood in zigzag queues to bathe before the tube-well. Inside Irfan's cozy home his mother was frying fish. His mother coaxed him with her soft, motherly voice to go and offer his prayer. The sweet smell of mustard oil invaded his being. He could hear the gurgling of his stomach. As he left his home that day, the sun was, how should I put it, the sun was shooting unfriendly rays onto land that was nothing but a forest of plastics.

The mosque was packed like an anthill. Irfan had little option than to find a place on the ground. The shaded part was already occupied. Just then he saw the commotion. Everybody was getting up. All was silent. The loudspeaker blared out a voice that was reciting verses in Arabic. He felt bored. It was difficult to follow what was happening.

"Just see what others are doing and follow them quietly," is how his mother had always helped when he complained of the difficulty.

It had perplexed him. He could not understand a single word except of course, *Allah-O-Akbar*, and even here the meaning did not emerge clearly. Akbar meant nothing to him. It was just a name of a Moghul King, that's all. He found that his photographic mind was busy imagining the fish his mother was preparing. The brown fried fish absorbed all his waking attention. He gulped his spit and felt his Adam's apple move up and down. Even before the prayer was officially over, he walked back to his home.

After that terrible Mamta Kulkarni incident, two things happened. Irfan swore not to play cricket but merely to watch it, and he wished to learn how to cook. But he soon discovered that living inside the home too was not easy. If man dominated the outer world, then woman was the absolute ruler of the home. The world, he realized at that young age, had no space for children like him who were troubled by both.

Discouraged from watching TV and banned from the kitchen, he felt trapped like a parrot in a circus ring.

Two days later, he located a new shop that was being constructed. Rumors were afloat that a new video-game parlor would be opened. Women with their child tied to their backs were climbing the bamboo stairs with bricks on their head. A week later, it was inaugurated by a local gangster, who had once rigged elections for Indira. He had arrived at the venue chewing betel leaf, and his breath smelled of whiskey. Soon, Irfan learned to play those American propaganda video games where a guerilla, a Sylvester Stallone look-alike is dropped from a helicopter and then goes about killing villagers. The video-game parlor soon turned into a hot spot. Simulated murder became the rage, the latest fashion among the boys. The shop smelled of human sweat and *ghutkas* all through the day and late night. Boys bunked their classes. They got trashed by their parents, but their newfound out love for the game would just not abate.

Within months, the number of gold chains that rolled over the often naked chest of the owner multiplied like the scales of an onion.

One day, an ordinary day, an extra-ordinary day, if you wish, Irfan arrived at the shop. He stood silently watching the others play. His pocket was torn and his hand empty. He suffered from consumerist dissatisfaction – a chronic ailment that afflicts everyone who lives in a thriving world of commerce. His sense of lack overwhelmed him. A sense of anger, coupled with acute Buddhist melancholy took hold of his poor, deprived heart. He felt like the famous cat from children's fable that tries very hard to get hold of the grapes, but is somehow unable to do so. Like the cat from the fable, he could only see the grapes from afar.

He walked the streets, up and down, like the young philosopher who discovered that the world is full of suffering. People are born, they suffer, and then they die a rat's death. After three hours of contemplation he discovered two things: (a) he did not have any money, (b) he must find a way to make some. At first, he thought of asking his aunt for some money. His plan was to gamble. But it was a risky affair. If he was caught, or if somebody sneaked the news to his mummy, he would be in a mess.

With tearful eyes, he stood at the gate of the parlor. Then he spotted a pair of old, haggard shoes. An idea suddenly struck him like a revelation that leaves you stunned. He knew that there was a shop near his home where one could sell the old shoes and get some four to five rupees. If he could persuade the owner to give him the shoes, he could sell them and share half the profit. With two rupees he could play twice. He doled out this idea to the owner. He agreed. Irfan took the shoes and walked toward the shop to sell them. As he walked, the images of the video game popped in his head. He kept imagining how he would kill the villagers, and what mistakes he should avoid, whom he should trust and, importantly, what route he should take. After he slays every one of them, should he burn their houses?

All things done, he reached the shop. He sold the shoe and received five rupees from the man. He promptly returned to the parlor. The owner was talking to a friend. When he saw Irfan, he could not believe his good luck. The guy did what he had promised to do. He took the coins from his hand, opened the drawer and slipped them in. Irfan could hear the clanking of the coins as they fell into the steel bowls. When Irfan asked for his share, the owner got up, inhaled the air, pumped his hairy Sunny Deol chest, took hold of Irfan by his collar and threw him out.

He fell on his aunt's feet and, like Buddha, he shed his maiden tears at the world of men and commerce.

Mamma I am not an atheist, I am a lover

ONE FINE morning Mr. Anandi received a phone call. The caller identified himself as "the Inspector from your *thana*" (police station).

"The *boro babu* wants to see you."

"Are you sure you are looking for me?" said Mr. Anandi.

He went straight to his superior and informed him about the matter. The superior heard him as one hears a paid dog. He took his permission and headed for the police station.

When he reached the Baranagore Police Station he saw much to his delight a cooler. He drank chilled water from the steel mug that was handcuffed to the cooler.

Mr. Anandi had thought all the while that it was a case of mistaken identity. Once he met the police officer, he would explain everything to him and go home. He stood like a donkey for almost three hours. He legs itched with pain.

Just to kill time he eyed the boy who stood behind the lock-up. Men, when held in chain, resemble animals, he thought.

But anyhow, the betel-leaf chewing police officer arrived. His belly was round as a globe. It was as if he had swallowed it.

It turned out that the Inspector was a smart ass. He did not beat about the bush. Instead he took out a diary. It was by a boy named Rakesh. He had just committed suicide, and according to police it was a "case of homo-love." This meant, in dignified parlance, a failed loved affair between two young men. The officer informed Mr. Anandi that his name appeared as many as twenty-seven times in the diary. It was clear enough that he was in a sexual relationship with Rakesh. He would file a case against him for abetment of suicide, which is a criminal offence. And yes, if possible he would also press charges for committing an unnatural offence. Sodomy is a criminal offence, he reminded Mr. Anandi.

Now these officers are so smart that they regularly issue threats, and based on the response they issue further threats. But if the accused were smart enough, he would know how to resolve the matter. He could say, for instance, that hence the officer's wife would no longer have to worry about her child's education and things like that.

If such things are said with appropriate formality, then usually the fate of the investigation is decided in favor of the accused. The balance of force shifts. But Mr. Anandi, being who he was, did not make any such offers.

Part 2. Extracts from the diary of Mr. Anandi

I don't know what love is. I cannot quite put it into words. He says that love is like a Sufi poem. The more you try to grasp it rationally, the more it evades you. You can't, after all, hold wet sand in your hands. Can you? Tell me! Is it possible to hold water? But there is one thing that one can know about love. It is this: love endows us with serenity, like watching a landscape does. When you are with your beloved, your life seems to move slowly. It is as if someone has just pressed a button, and the movie of your life, in which you act, moves in slow motion. I love this experience. You tend to live each moment, you eat properly, you dress properly. You tend to love yourself and bestow all respects that hitherto you had deemed unfit and useless.

~ ~ ~ ~

I saw him today in the library of the British Council. He was buried in a mountain of books. For almost twenty minutes he did not once move his eyes off the paper. My god, I had never seen anyone reading with such devotion. I knew right then and there that he was a writer; a dreamy poet. Even before our eyes could meet, I had fallen head over heels in love with him. I wanted so badly to fall on his lap like Menoka from the fairytale and disturb him. Gosh I so badly started missing him right from that moment. I felt like an unemployed youth who while searching for a job ends up finding a Kohinoor.

~ ~ ~ ~

I have read almost everything he has written for the blogs. I love him doubly now. My love for him has soared like the points of Sensex.

~ ~ ~ ~

Today I woke up very early in the morning. I could hear the cry of a rooster and whistle of a train. I lay on the bed for almost two hours. I kept changing my posture. All the while I was imagining various things that I was doing to him. While my eyes stared at the white ceiling, my filmy mind busily manufactured lovemaking scenes. Now, for the sake of decency, imagine this scene with me. There is a table. Two chairs. It is a cafeteria with big wide windows facing the blue mountain of Kurseong. In the distance the mountains rise and fall, one behind another. The snow-capped summit of Kanchenjunga is soaked in orange. The carpet is faded red. He is reading a book by Noam Chomsky and I am sipping my café. He gets up decisively like a whale rises from the depths of the ocean. He leaves the book on the table, holds my hand firmly and drags me into a room. We make love without using condom. We sit and smoke a post-sex cigarette. He makes perfect circle of smoke and releases them from his mouth. I try and fail. We laugh. The windowpane shakes…

~ ~ ~ ~

I read his article today. He says what a fucked up place this world is. Capital intervenes everywhere; be it a man peeing in a paid public toilet or a man making love. If you have no money, you can neither pee, nor can you fuck. It is this simple.

~ ~ ~ ~

I feel that his theories on social change and all that are very well. But who can change a world that rewards the status quo?

~ ~ ~ ~

The title of one of his stories is: Mamma I am not an atheist, I am a lover.

~ ~ ~ ~

In one of his essays on Tolstoy he writes, "It is a great paradox that while the rich Tolstoy accumulated wealth, the poor one distributed it." I am going to read Tolstoy. I hope I get the time to do so. I am so lazy when it comes to reading.

~ ~ ~ ~

When one visits a paradise, one must have a pen and a notebook. This way one can create a paradise within a paradise. This again is the first line that he wrote in a story that I just read today. God this guy is simply mad. And I am mad. And everybody is mad. Ummm I so love him.

~~~~

Part 3

Hi there! This is me. Your boy, who lives next door with his mother, an aging father, and a spoiled cat! The portion of diary that I quoted above was showed to me by Mr. Anandi. He was sent to me by a well-meaning editor of a gay magazine, *The Pink Pages,* to which I had contributed in the past.

The morning I first met Mr. Anandi, it was unusually cold. As you know well, Kolkata is a hot and humid city. We experience things such as snow only in our dreams. That morning, we sat down in my home. I was listening to him, and as he spoke I could see vapor rise from his mouth. The following is an excerpt of the conversation that took place between me and my character.

"A… Hi! I am so sorry that I had to keep you like this for about (I check my watch) twenty minutes or so."

"No, really it is okay. I have been sent to you by Harish Bhai. He thinks you can help me."

"I'll do everything possible. Everything that is within the reach of an ordinary lawyer."

When I said this, he looked a bit reassured. He sat there rolling his eyes, looking at the books that were stacked on the walls.

"You too, like Rakesh, read a lot of books, I see," he said after a while.

"Yes. One cannot survive without reading," I said and smiled softly like a perfect reader of books.

"Can I ask you one thing?" he said.

"Sure."

"I am told that you are secretly writing a collection of short stories. Could you not include our story in it?" he said.

I felt uneasy. I mean no one had ever asked me like this. It wasn't as if this guy meant any harm to me. But still how could I write about that which I am not.

Doubts began to rise in my mind. Could I actually write such a short story? Would it be convincing? Will anyone ever bother to read it? Will it bore the reader? And most importantly, will I be able to pull off the story?

Here I fell silent. I could neither say a frank yes nor a no. I somehow did not want to hurt him. So I kept shuffling this idea in my head.

You know, writing a story is no easy business. Unless a story calls you, you can do nothing much. I think it is not just authors who decide what stories they can write. The story itself decides the author. With these half-formed thoughts that were trying their best to come out of their gestation, I walked the street.

It was evening and I noticed absentmindedly a small function of the *Vishwa Hindu Parishad* (World Hindu Council, VHP) being held in the south part of our city. The crowd was thin. Barring a few retired old men and women, it was empty. These were largely people from the other side of Bengal's border who had been displaced due to waves of racial cleansing at the hands of Muslim fundamentalists.

That same evening I met my girlfriend Aditi. I said to her everything about Mr. Anandi, his sexual orientation that had been unnecessarily problematized by the law, his boyfriend's sudden suicide, the impending criminal charges against him, the demands of the police officers. She listened to me quietly while she cooked fish with curd.

I sat later with the plan to write a first draft. Normally, I am never hesitant. As a writer I am that dog who bites into every morsel that comes its way. I had thought through the story well in advance. I would write a story in which I appear as a lawyer, I seek my girlfriend's advice, Mr. Anandi would commit suicide in my short story. I had decided not to introduce too many new facts. It would be an honest, straightforward tale of what happened to Mr. Anandi.

I had hardly authored two pages when I received a call early in the morning. It was from the hospital. Mr. Anandi had actually attempted to commit suicide. I rushed to the hospital with guilt in my head. Somehow I was blaming myself for all this.

By the time I reached the hospital I was told that he was dead. I fell on the chair and sobbed for a long while.

The Story of Sufi Alif
Who Fell in Love with Books and a Sultana

(A story for children)

ONCE UPON a time, yes, once upon a time, it so happened that a Sufi named Alif fell in love with a black-eyed Sultana. It was said of the Sultana that the Sultan of the Kingdom, who himself had dozens of begums, on seeing her, had ordered that the Sultana be presented to him on the night of *Eid-ul-Fitr*.

So the imperial guards arrived at her palace and stood below it. It looked arrestingly beautiful, especially because of the special crescent-shaped white-blue moon. The moon was crowned with a circle of yellow, red and orange light.

The red walls of the palace stood littered with yellow-red torches of flame that surrounded it.

The Sultana, much to the astonishment of the guards, refused to go.

"Go and tell your stupid Sultan that he cannot have all his subjects, just as fancy pleases him. There are certain norms of decency that women like me like to observe."

The message was relayed. And it added to the stature of the Sultana, who had dared to refuse her Sultan. After this she won considerable fame for her courage.

Our Alif, the one who is very soon going to fall in love with her, was a recluse of sorts. Each afternoon as men rushed to participate in what they called affairs of life, he sat down solemnly to read books. He liked doing nothing better than to read the books, until the evening when the sky, as seen from his window, changed its color from blue to luminous red-yellow-orange, and the sound of Azan filtered through his window. Out of habit or because of the noise, he would stop reading his book and wait for the Muazin to come to an end.

Years ago, one afternoon while he was reading a book inside the deserted library, he felt suddenly that his body had become light as a feather or as the sunlight that filtered through the widow. The words that emanated from the pages had formed whole, sequentially arranged thoughts. For a fleeting while, he felt as if he had realized something strange about human existence, something that only he knew and understood. The light was blinding, and a sharp spasm, a feeling of spacelessness and timelessness took hold of him. It was akin to the feeling of masturbation. For these few seconds he thought he had lost his body, as if it had merged with a mysterious power that was far beyond his rational comprehension. Even if I die now I won't have a regret. He paused to think over this line that crossed his mind, then his face became covered with his god-like serene smile.

Reading, he had discovered at a very young age, "cleanses the soul, purifies it and uplifts it from baseness." As he stood staring at the blank sky, he dictated this to one of his pupils.

"And those who don't read end up becoming nothing. Yes, write the word three times," he said again.

"Because we don't recognize ourselves in others, our people have been unable to recognize others in themselves. And this is the reason why our entire civilization has fallen into disuse like rotten garbage."

Every week, despite his otherworldly ways of being, he would adopt the path of those who are given to ways of worldly men. Reading had made him weak. Yes it had. If you were to take a knife and tear his heart, all you would get to see are pages of countless books – all, yes, all of them laden with pus from his heart. There were so many tales in each book, so many books in each tale, intertwined like roots of trees. He knew very well that he would carry most of them to his grave. He would drink, fornicate with cheap old toothless whores, cry like school children on their laps, spend the night with well-known drug addicts, gamblers and come back home and sleep peacefully besides his frail mother with whom he lived.

One afternoon, drunk to the hilt, he was walking the street accompanied by his shadow and a dog. The gong of the church filled the air. It was two in the afternoon, when the bazaars are deserted. Two emaciated men bearing a palanquin appeared in the turning of the road. Soon, the whole palanquin with eight bearers walked the bazaar. Their feet marched in unison like those of a caterpillar.

Behind the neat white curtain, he caught her maiden glimpse. He fell into the grip of a strong animal-like urge to walk closer to her, smell her body, touch her. But certain rules of decency apply to everyone, whether they are Sufis or traders. Besides, our Sufi was no lecher. He knew that to get her, to be hers would mean that he would wait for her. He left the place as soon as he could, as he had to take his classes of grammar, geometry and political science.

That evening he reached his hut and sat below the gigantic mango tree that had been washed with the golden rays of the dying sun. The sweet smell of fresh mango greeted him as he sat down for the day's lesson. Just as a good *pir* knows the heart of his pupils, so do good pupils know the heart of their *pir*. One of them, a certain young boy who was trying to find a way to explain to a blind man what a color is, asked the Sufi if everything was alright. The Sufi responded by uttering a few inaudible words. It settled the matter. The pupil thought it best not to inquire any further. Another pupil who had the ability to separate watercolors nodded with his head to leave the Master. After the lesson was over, the Sufi sat down in his home to write down what exactly had happened to him. He wrote almost everything about himself in his private diary. He thought sincerely that the medicinal quality of writing might heel his wounds. And it did. Writing alone had helped him. It alone had prevented him from plunging into the vicious cycle of anguish that all young writers are prone to experience. He had found that the printed word alone could provide that shadow everyone needs.

He kept his notebook after scribing a few words and lay on his cot. He stayed there for three days. His pupils were so worried that they invited the *hakim* to come and see him.

The doctor, after he studied his patient, said, "I am unable to comprehend the hidden affliction of this man. Had he been an ordinary man, I could possibly have suggested that he spend time with women: if not one then several dozens of them. But he is a philosopher."

"How do I heal him?" he asked in a straightforward manner and looked at his students for an answer.

No one spoke. His pupil, the one who was busy formulating a mathematical equation to prove God's existence asked the doctor politely to come with him till the gate.

The disciples knew not what to do. They prayed for their *pir*, recited verses from the holy book, and they often took him to the Ganges, which they believe purifies one's soul. On the fifth day, seized by an inner urge, he asked his pupil to scribe his words on the blank white paper. Man was mud, both, before and after he became a man, he dictated.

"Write it down Nazim, son, write it down" he said as his right hand was playing with his snow-white beard and he was walking up and down in his room, which had chalk-white walls and transparent cotton curtains.

Now, there are three different stories concerning him. We shall have the good fortune to learn each one of them.

It was an evening when the faithful were busy offering their prayer in a mosque. The smell of incense stick hung in the air. Alif appeared, walking in the street with his head on his hand. Street dogs, incensed by the smell of fresh blood, or perhaps because of a sense of empathy, followed him. These dogs, after all, knew the inner torments of those who are possessed with love or hatred.

The dogs walked behind the Sufi. The Sufi was followed by the dogs. The Sufi reached the crossing of the roads. The Sufi stood still. The dogs stood still. Another group of dogs appeared, and they followed him. Thus, he reached the palace of the Sultana.

The Sultana saw him from her window and was so deeply moved at the sight that she immediately renounced the world. Henceforth, she was to beg, wander like an animal and pursue the forgotten ways of being in the world. In the course of several years, she is reported to have authored several anthologies of her lyrical outbursts. I have perused them, and quite frankly I find a lot of merit in them. I am fully convinced that as a work of art, they require our attention. I have also been informed by a good friend, who is an academic, that she could not have authored these works. The reason – what is the reason – it is pretty simple. She could not have written the couplets, as "those couplets have probably been sung by peasants from the lower class in far-flung places that she never visited all her life."

"And further, all this story about the Sultana writing such profound literary work is a sham which comes to us from the Court Historians. I have perused several documents by people who were not historians. They were travelers and merchants. And they all seem to agree with me. Some of them have recorded these same songs, but they ascribe the authorship to no one in particular. The Court at her time was scandalized, so much so, that in order to restore what in our time is called public relations, it proclaimed her as a divine poet."

There is another story.

According to this one, the Sultana did not see the Sufi from the window but, rather, from a breath-close distance. It was she who had opened the door, only to find her tormented beloved. It is widely believed that just then, there was a cyclone. Both rose up in the air like blades of grass. Only one man saw this improbable incident, and he went blind after that.

According to another legend, the Sultana saw from her mind's eye that the Sufi was walking toward her. She calmly opened the door and read the holy book, which soothed her beloved. She then placed back on his neck the head that had been severed, and both of them lived happily.

When I had narrated the above story to my three nieces, Sadaf, Shafat and Simran, they sat before me with silent eyes. It was a dark and starless night. Their mother had gone to the hospital to take care of a neighbor who had just attempted suicide, all because of a failed love affair.

A friend from the neighbor who had seen the women had reported to me that, "you should have seen how she was bleeding." And then he added on his own, "it was like a fish bleeding on the white marble floor."

I had innocently asked if she had slit open her wrist. To which he smiled like Shylock and said, "No no. She slit her wind pipe open with the knife."

I had to stay with my terrified nieces. My brother-in-law had been posted out of station due to election-related work. So, short of stories, and to divert their minds, I had recited to them a story that I had written.

Simran who is the oldest of them, broke out saying, "Mamu what do you think must have happened? We know that you don't believe in god or ghosts, so there is no point by which you can bring your rational self to believe all of this shit."

Children grow, and they ask questions that often leave one speechless. I had always heard other people say this. But today it was my turn.

I thought it over for a good while. Frankly what would the Sultana have done if she had seen the Sufi like that! I thought. I thought over my thoughts.

But then, to bring the day's business to a fair conclusion, I said, "Well, if you ask me, then as a lawyer who cannot believe anything that is spurious or suspicious, I think that the Sultana would probably have fainted on seeing her beloved standing before her door with his head on his hand. And who wouldn't?"

All of us then burst into childish laughter.

www.ingramcontent.com/pod-product-compliance
Lightning Source LLC
Chambersburg PA
CBHW041413010726

47507CB00005B/260